"Just put up your gun, real easy.

Lay it on the bar, and that'll be the end of it," Kinkaid said.

"You know that ain't so, marshal."

"Have it your way."

Slayton shook his head. "No sir. We'll have it your way. That'll be just fine."

He wiggled his fingers to loosen them, then went for it. Kinkaid was a lot faster. He put one in Deak Slayton's chest, just above the third shirt button. Deak slid down the front of the bar, leaving a long, dark, shiny smear on the wood. In the dim lamplight, it looked almost like creosote.

Deak swallowed once, then a small bubble of blood ballooned between his lips. He groaned, the rush of air bursting the bubble. Then it got quiet.

BILL DUGAN
GUN PLAY AT CROSS CREEK

HarperPaperbacks
A Division of HarperCollinsPublishers

This is a work of fiction. The characters, incidents, and dialogues are products of the author's imagination and are not to be construed as real. Any resemblance to actual events or persons, living or dead, is entirely coincidental.

HarperPaperbacks   *A Division of* HarperCollins*Publishers*
10 East 53rd Street, New York, N.Y. 10022

Copyright © 1990 by Bill Dugan
All rights reserved. No part of this book may be used or reproduced in any manner whatsoever without written permission of the publisher, except in the case of brief quotations embodied in critical articles and reviews. For information address HarperCollins*Publishers,*
10 East 53rd Street, New York, N.Y. 10022.

Cover art by Miro

First HarperPaperbacks printing: August 1990

Printed in the United States of America

HarperPaperbacks and colophon are trademarks of HarperCollins*Publishers*

10 9 8 7 6 5 4 3 2

CHAPTER 1

The sign said "Cross Creek" in sickly blue paint. The letters were uneven, done in a shaky hand, like that of a child still uncomfortable with the alphabet. Under the name of the town, much smaller, but no less shaky, was the legend "pop. 879—last count." Someone had added the last two words, as a joke, most likely, and the lettering was bold and straight. The sign had been there for six years. The legend was much more recent, added by one of the saner souls who had decided Cross Creek was not much of a place to visit, and sure as hell was no place to live. The town, in short, had a bad reputation.

Cross Creek sat in the heart of Wyoming cattle country, and its reputation did nothing to discourage visits from hands of the two dozen or so huge spreads that fanned out across the Laramie foothills.

They wanted a place to drink, and a place to dip their wicks. Cross Creek never let them down. Nobody left thirsty, and nobody left horny.

But the town also wanted to grow, or at least to survive. Its more civilized residents were getting tired of the Friday night shoot outs, brawling knife fights that spilled out of the saloons, of which there were currently six, and into the streets. They were tired of stepping over smelly drunks on the way to church, of which they had their choice of two, on a Sunday morning. They wanted normal lives. They wanted the kind of quiet town they had imagined when they left the Ohio Valley and the slums of St. Louis, the stockyards of Chicago, and the mines of Pennsylvania. In short, they wanted Cross Creek to be decent, a place to raise a family, a place to rock on the front porch after a hard day's work. A place to die. Quietly. In bed.

But the cowboys thought differently. Deak Slayton thought differently as he rode past the sign one summer Friday evening, with a half-dozen men from the Rocking Y. He reined in abruptly, backed his horse up, and stared at the sign, leaning forward from his saddle and squinting into the red ball of the settting sun. He'd seen the sign before, two or three dozen times at least.

"Come on, Deak, the hell you lookin' at?" Riley Grand shouted, jerking his own mount in a half circle and tilting his hat back on his head. Grand was thirsty, he had a month's pay in his jeans, and only sixty hours to spend it all.

"Nothing," Slayton said. He pointed at the sign, but didn't say anything else.

"What about it? It's a sign. You seen it before."

"Yeah, I seen it before." But this time something about it just got on Deak Slayton's nerves. He'd had a bad week, and he was hot, tired, and, above all else, angry, with that abiding anger that is so deeply rooted it seems that nothing will ever expunge it. He jerked his Colt out of its holster and cocked the hammer.

"The hell you doin', Deak? Come on."

"Hold your water. I'm thinking."

"That ought to make the papers back East. Maybe an Extra, even."

"You got a big mouth, Riley," Slayton said. Then he squeezed the trigger. The bullet pierced the sign just below the "o" in "Cross." Slayton grinned. "Looks a damn sight better that way, you ask me."

Grand wasn't so sure. "I think that new marshal they got in town might think different on that, Deak. You better put that gun up."

"Don't bother me. I seen lots of men wear a badge didn't have the legs to carry it when it came time."

"That ain't what I hear about this 'un."

"A marshal's a marshal, Riley. My daddy killed one once, back in El Paso. I ain't been scared of one since then."

"I'm telling you, Deak, this one's different. He ain't like that."

"Maybe so. But if he ain't, he's the first one." In quick succession, Slayton fired three more times. When he finally holstered the Colt, he grinned at Riley Grand through a cloud of gunsmoke. The sign lay on the ground in pieces. Even the post had been shattered. It looked like someone had hit it a good lick with an axe.

Grand turned his horse and kicked it with his spurs. The animal leapt forward, and the rest of the hands followed him, except for Slayton, who sat there grinning at his handiwork. When the corners of his mouth got tired, he nudged his mount with his knees and moved on into Cross Creek at a walk.

They spotted the others already on foot, crossing the street and heading for The Hangin' Tree, a saloon, cum hotel, noted for its unwatered whiskey and unwashed women, the two things in life Deak Slayton couldn't get enough of.

He dismounted at the hitching rail in front of The Hangin' Tree, tied off, and stomped up onto the splintery boardwalk. Instead of going in right away, he dropped onto a wooden bench, also splintery, and every bit as much in need of paint as the boardwalk or, for that matter, the saloon itself, and rolled a cigarette.

He was already licking the paper when he saw someone watching him from across the street. The man's face was half hidden by his hat brim, but there was no mistaking the glitter on his chest. The brightly polished metal caught the rays of a declining sun and glowed like a ruby star.

Slayton finished licking the paper, tapped both ends of the new cigarette on his heel a little too hard, and shoved one end into his mouth. He leaned back, flicked a match with his thumbnail, and took a long drag, tilting his hat back on his head as he let the smoke out in a thick gray rope.

The marshal didn't say anything. And he didn't

move, just stood there watching. Slayton started a
wave, then thought it might be pushing things.
There was something about the man behind the red
star that made his blood freeze a little. He took
another drag on the cigarette, blew the smoke out
through his nose this time, then stubbed it out on
the boardwalk.

The marshal stepped down into the street and
walked toward him, pushing his fancy jacket back
off his hip. Slayton saw the gun, and was surprised
at how ordinary it looked. Just a plain Colt, with
dark brown grips. No pearl handle, no silver plate.
Just a good, serviceable weapon. He would have
expected something more showy from a hot shot.

The marshal planted one foot on the boardwalk. "You don't like our sign, I hear."

Slayton didn't say anything.

The marshal watched him closely for a moment
before continuing. "In fact, I hear we don't even
have a sign anymore, you didn't like it so much.
That true?"

Slayton lit another cigarette, blew a long plume
of smoke in the marshal's direction, and remained
silent.

The marshal waved at the smoke. He smiled,
but just barely. "Never did like smoking," he said.
"It's a bad habit. But then, some folks just never get
the message. You know what I mean?"

Slayton finally broke his silence. "Marshal, you
got something to say to me, why not say it flat out?"

The marshal shook his head. "I said about all
I'm gonna say, Deak. Except for one thing..." He
waited for Slayton to ask.

The cowhand didn't want to ask, but knew the marshal would tell him anyway, so he said, "What's that?"

"Funny you should ask," the marshal said. "I expect that sign will be back in place before morning. Not the same one, of course, but one just as good. Henessey's General Store carries everything a fellow could need. Wood, nails, paint. I guess you could even get a paintbrush, you need one. You just pass the word, in case you happen to bump into anybody might know something about what happened to that sign."

"I'll do that, Marshal."

The marshal nodded, touched the brim of his hat with the tips of two fingers, then turned and walked back across the street. Deak Slayton glanced at the gun on his hip, thought about reaching for it a second, then thought better of it. The Colt had already got him in enough hot water, and he hadn't even had a drink yet. He looked at the marshal's back, then realized he was being watched. Just past the marshal's shoulder, he could see the marshal's face staring back at him in the store window across the street.

The marshal smiled, but it was a cold smile.

Deak Slayton sat there for a while, wondering how the marshal knew it was he who had blown the sign all to hell. He hadn't been that far behind Riley and the others. And there wasn't anybody else out there, not that he saw, anyway. He decided it must have been Riley Grand and his big mouth again. The marshal probably heard the shooting, asked Riley about it when he rode in, and Riley must have told him.

He'd have to talk to Riley about that big mouth of his. Again. But it could wait till later, after he had a drink. It had been too long already, nearly five weeks, since his last taste of whiskey. It was about time. As he stood up, he saw the marshal leaning in the open doorway of the *Cross Creek Courier*, the county newspaper, across the way. The sun was behind the row of buildings across the way now, a dark red bulge just visible over the rooftops. That side of the street was in shadow. Under his hat brim, the marshal's face was in deeper shadow still.

Slayton couldn't tell for sure whether the marshal was watching him, or just watching. Deak felt a little shiver run up his back, and he moved a little faster than he had intended, shoving the double doors of The Hangin' Tree open with his elbows and letting them fan closed with a squeak of hinges.

He spotted Riley Grand right away, leaning on the bar and laughing about something, flapping his gums to a couple of hands from the Flying V spread. Ginny was there, too, hanging on every word. She looked good, better than usual, in fact. The red dress made her shoulders look even whiter than he remembered.

Ginny looked at him and took a step his way, excused herself and danced across the floor toward him. Maybe she was tired of listening to Riley, he thought. The man does go on. When she reached him, she threw her arms around him and stood on tiptoe. Deak was tall, nearly six two, and he had to lean down to plant a kiss on Ginny's forehead.

She squeezed him, then said, "You shouldn't do that, Deak. Not here. I mean, everybody's looking at us."

Slayton laughed. "If not here, where?"

Ginny squeezed him again. "You know what I mean."

"What's Riley on about?"

"Oh, you know Riley."

"Yeah, I do," he said.

She backed away a step. There was something in his voice she didn't like. "What's wrong, Deak?"

"Nothing a drink won't cure," he said. "Buy you one?"

She nodded. He led the way, planting himself on Riley Grand's elbow, up against the bar.

"Took you so long, Deak?" Riley asked, sliding over a bit to make room for him.

"Had a little talk with the new marshal."

"Brad, here, was just tellin' me about him," Riley said. "He's a bad one."

"So he led me to believe," Deak said, not really wanting to talk about it. He turned to the bartender. "Donny, let me and the little lady have a bourbon apiece, would you?"

He was getting thirstier by the minute. It seemed like a good night to get drunk. Rub a little felt off his antlers. Hell, maybe even have another talk with the new marshal. He'd be damned if he was going to worry about the damn sign.

CHAPTER 2

Morgan Atwater reined in. He leaned over the saddle and looked at the splintered remains of the sign on the ground. His practiced eye picked out the neat, round edges of the bullet holes. The board had fractured along its grain, but there was no mistaking what had caused the splitting. He shook his head, less in wonder than in sadness. Some trigger-happy fool had taken out a world of disillusionment on a piece of wood. Atwater hoped whoever it was felt better, but knew it wouldn't last.

Squeezing his mount with his knees, he coaxed the big bay into a slow trot. The town looked like a thousand others he had seen. Its buildings all one or two stories except for one, most sun-bleached timber or stark white paint. They looked like they could have been picked up from someplace in

Texas, or Nebraska or . . . what the hell was the difference? He wasn't here for the architecture. As he moved closer, the setting sun filled all their windows with bloody light, and they stared back at him like dozens of bleary-eyed drunks.

But Atwater was used to scrutiny, used to hostility too, for all of that. Cross Creek had nothing to offer he hadn't seen before. Except for one. And that one thing was the reason he was here at all. He wasn't about to be spooked by some harebrained would-be gunslinger. And he didn't give a damn how many disapproving glances stabbed him in the back. He was used to that, too.

At the edge of town he slowed his horse, letting it walk down the center of the main street. Cross Creek looked busy, but that was to be expected. Friday nights in cow country were safety valves. Most Fridays, cowhands blew off as much steam as they could, sometimes a little more, dropped most of their cash, and stumbled back to business on a Monday morning. When that Friday coincided with the end of the month, rowdiness became a way of life.

He spotted a sign advertising a livery stable, and nudged his horse a little faster, checking the shops and saloons on both sides of the street. The place didn't look half bad. There was even a newspaper. Maybe somebody around here can even read, he thought, smiled at the notion, and clucked to the big bay again. It had been a long ride, and he was dead tired.

He dismounted in front of the stable. The sign said "Milton's Livery," and it looked as if it had been recently painted. That meant either a thriving business or a new one. He hoped the former as he tugged on the reins and pulled the bay through the yawning doors. Inside, a pair of coal-oil lamps smeared orange light on the packed dirt and straw litter. A stack of hay bales looked like huge blocks of bullion in one corner.

A wrinkled little man, bits of straw clinging to his pants and sticking out of his white hair, dropped a hayfork and stepped out of an open stall. He shuffled toward Atwater, his face a question mark.

Atwater nodded. The little man ignored him, walked around the horse once, his gnarled fingers patting its flank, and, when he had completed the circuit, said, "Nice horse, mister."

"Thanks," Atwater said.

"You should take better care of him, though. Looks like you been riding him too hard."

"I come a long way."

"Don't matter. You kill this big fella, you walk back, don't you . . ." It wasn't a question, and Atwater didn't even try to answer. He waited for the little man to continue.

He did. "I can get him back to the kinda shape he should be in, though. If you stay long enough."

"I plan to."

"Good. Only right a man should take care of the beasts he depends on."

Atwater smiled. He'd seen all kinds of men, but by far the most opinionated, by type, were neither ministers nor politicians, the two most likely choices. They were stablemen. More often than not they had the manners of a rattler and the charm of a dead cow. But if you found one who knew horses, you were ahead of the game.

"What do you charge?" Atwater asked.

"Ten dollars the month. Three dollars the week. Four bits the day. Your choice."

Atwater fished in his pocket, pulled out a ten-dollar gold piece, and flipped it in the air. The little man snatched it with reflexes of a man half his age. He glanced at the coin. "This for a month, or you want change?"

"No change."

The old man finally introduced himself. "John Milton," he said, sticking out a gnarled hand more like a claw. "No relation."

"Relation to whom?"

"You know, *Paradise Lost*, the poet."

"Not much for poetry," Atwater said.

"Me neither. But I always tell people. Some folks ask, and I got tired of hearing the same old jokes. So I tell 'em up front, no relation. Saves time. Course, telling you how I save time don't save none, do it?" he cackled, tucked the gold piece in his shirt, and grabbed the reins.

"There a good hotel in town?" Atwater asked.

"You mean a hotel hotel or you mean a hotel henhouse?"

"A hotel hotel, I guess."

"Nope."

"How about a clean hotel henhouse, then?"

"Nope."

"*Is* there a hotel of any kind in town?"

"Down the block. Never stayed there myself, but I guess it's alright. Never heard no complaints, anyhow. Course, it *is* the only one in town so what would be the point?"

Atwater thanked the old man and backed toward the yawning doors. The sun was breathing its last gasp as he stepped into the street and turned. He looked up at the sky. Huge smears of pink, purple, and whitish oranges stretched from horizon to horizon. He loved sunset more than any other time of day. This one was good but not spectacular. As he lowered his gaze, the jagged peaks of the Laramie range, almost black as coal now, sawed the sky in half.

All in all, he thought, not a bad little town. Nice place to raise a family. But that part hurt, and he pushed it away. It wouldn't do to get his hopes up. Not just yet, anyway.

He could hear a racket coming from up the block, half like a party and half like a riot. As he drew closer, he realized it was coming from The Hangin' Tree. Atwater wasn't in the mood for any loud noise, and it sounded like the cowhands in that particular saloon were fixing to wake the dead, so he moved on past. He wondered whether he'd be able to sleep in the place, since the saloon was right under most of the hotel rooms.

But first things first. There were two other saloons in town, neither one of which called attention to itself. Either one would do just fine.

He drank only beer now, hadn't had a whiskey in more than eight years. Eight years and four months, to be exact, he thought. And seventeen days. He smiled at the precision. Like everything else he did, he paid attention to details when it came to his drinking. Wasn't crazy about beer, either, didn't like the taste of it. But that was good. He drank less that way. And that's the way he wanted it.

Atwater started angling across the street. The doors of The Hangin' Tree snapped open. Atwater turned. His gun was out before the flying body had even cleared the boardwalk. He felt a little foolish, pulling his Colt to shoot down a flying drunkard, but that was part of his life, too. It kept him alive, that gun, and the one thing he knew for certain was that if you weren't sure whether to draw or not, you shouldn't even pack a gun.

He watched the airborne cowhand land heavily on his back, slide off the boardwalk into the dirt, and lay there panting. Atwater holstered his Colt again and turned away. He heard the doors fly open again, but this time he didn't bother to turn around.

He'd had too many fights with drunks as it was. They were always spoiling for one, and if somebody whipped them, they usually went looking for somebody they could whip themselves. That's how it was, because nobody liked to lose. Not even Morgan Atwater. But he wasn't in the mood for a fight, with fists or anything else. That wasn't why he'd come to Cross Creek, and if he had anything to say about it, that's how it would be.

He was already on the opposite boardwalk when he realized someone was calling to him. He glanced over his shoulder. In the illuminated rectangle on the ground, he saw the cowhand struggling to get up. The man was shouting something incoherent, obviously aimed at him, but he ignored it.

Stepping through the doors to the saloon, he moved to a corner and sat down at a table. The bartender watched him quietly. "Beer, please," Atwater said.

The bartender nodded, drew the beer, and sliced the foamy hood off it with a wooden blade. He shoved it to the front edge of the nicked old bar and Atwater got up slowly to go and retrieve it.

He slid a silver dollar across the bar, waited for his change, then lugged the thick glass mug back to his table. He took off his hat and shook out his long hair, dropped the hat on the table, and took a long, single pull on the beer. Wiping his mustache on his sleeve, he leaned back in his chair and stared at himself in the mirror.

Morgan Atwater didn't much like what he saw. His dark brown hair was getting a little thin. There was a point over his forehead where it had receded on either side. His sideburns were kind of scraggly, with just a hint of gray. His mustache was too long, and a little grayer than the sideburns. Not quite salt and pepper, there was still the evidence of a few years in it.

His skin was taut and the muscles of his jaw were hard knots. His hands, too, were hard. Thick knuckles, ropey veins networking their backs and running on up to his elbows, where the thick forearms disappeared in his trail-dusted sleeves.

He looked exactly like what he was, a no longer quite so young man who had done more than his share of hard traveling. The blue eyes were bright and sharp, and lively enough that they made him look a handful of years younger than he was. At forty-one, he had a few miles on him, enough for a couple of lives if the truth were known.

The beer was warm, and not quite as bitter as that he was used to back in Texas. The Germans liked theirs strong, and a little too thick for his taste. Staring at himself in the mirror, he wondered why he had come. He knew the answer, but it didn't quite persuade him anymore. He was beginning to think it was a hare brained scheme, one he would come to regret. He was still wondering when the door flew open.

The same cowhand he'd last seen covered with dust in the street was standing there with his hands on his hips. The man was more than a little drunk, there was no doubt about that. He wavered from side to side as he tried to appear sober, but his face was flushed and his eyes watery.

"You," he said.

Atwater ignored him.

"I'm talkin' to you, cowboy," the drunk said again.

Atwater turned to look at him, but still didn't respond.

"Deak, you best get on home," the bartender said.

"Not talkin' to you, Charlie. Talkin' to the drifter, there. Looks like he don't hear so good, though."

"Deak, I'm not tellin' you again." Charlie reached under the bar and jerked out a sawed-off shotgun. He set it down on the bar, making sure it cracked hard on the wood. It was the only noise in the bar. The handful of patrons sat quietly, their

eyes moving from Charlie to the man in the doorway and back.

"Don't need that mare's leg, Charlie. I got no
quarrel with you."

"You got no quarrel with anybody, Deak. Not
in my saloon, you don't."

"I ain't askin' you, Charlie."

Atwater's eyes flicked past Deak's shoulder and
the cowhand, drunk as he was, still noticed it. He
turned to see the marshal pushing open the doors.

"This is more like it," Deak said.

CHAPTER 3

The marshal shoved the door aside and stood with his legs spread. At-water noticed the marshal's coat, pinned behind his hip. He didn't like it.

"Deak," the marshal said. "You been making a pure pain of yourself all evening. I think it's about time we put a stop to it."

Slayton teetered unsteadily. He tried to turn, lost his balance momentarily, regained it, and stood bobbing and weaving as he tried to stay upright. "Marshal," he said, "this ain't none of your affair."

"What do you want here, Deak?"

"Want a drink."

"You already had too much. Man can't hold his liquor shouldn't have any, don't you think that's true."

"I think you should go mind your marshaling

business. Whatever the hell that is." He laughed, but the sound of it was brittle, tinny. No one joined him, and his head rocked from side to side as he turned around to look at the bartender and the other patrons. "Ain't that right?"

The question was addressed to no one in particular, and the silence grew thicker still as no one bothered to answer. Deak staggered toward Atwater's table. He leaned heavily on it and lowered his face until he was even with Atwater. "Like I was saying," Deak said. "How come you didn't answer me when I was talkin' to you out there." Slayton threw his hand out wildly, knocking himself off balance, and he fell to one knee.

"Deak," the marshal said, "now, I'm not gonna tell you again. I think you better come along with me."

Slayton shook his head. "Can't do it, Marshal. Plain can't do it. Got no reason to be pushing me like this. I ain't done nothing. 'Sides, this man's gonna buy me a drink." Swiveling his head back, he stared at Atwater. "Ain't you?" he asked.

Atwater smiled. "You mind your manners, maybe I just might, Mr. Slayton."

The cowboy turned and addressed the room at large. "You all hear that? The man called me mister. Now I wonder how come? Why you think it is? Nobody else ever done that. Either he's got more manners than you all, or else he's about scared of me. Now which do you think it is." He looked at the marshal, who glared back at him but without answering.

Morgan watched the marshal. His name was

Brett Kinkaid. Kinkaid was about an inch or two above medium height. He was slender, but in a wiry way, and there was a little touch of the dandy in him. His boots were elaborately tooled, in Mexico by the look of them. The price of his coat would have clothed a family of four with more modest taste. His tie was clamped up under a starched collar with an ornate silver clasp studded with squarish hunks of polished turquoise.

Only his gun was ordinary-looking. That, and the lean, almost hungry-looking face. There was a touch of the lobo, maybe the coyote, since it lacked the wolf's nobility, and his mustache was sparse and jet-black. His cheeks were somewhat sunken, which made his cheekbones more prominent, giving him something of an Indian look, although his nose was too English for that to be accurate.

But it was the eyes that Morgan noticed most. They were hard as little lumps of obsidian. They glittered, but there was no warmth in the light, and not much intelligence. The gleam was more predatory than that, as if there were a snake or a crow somewhere in his lineage.

And all the while Morgan watched him, Kinkaid never took his eyes off Deak Slayton. Finally, the cowboy pounded a fist on the table. "You buying me a drink, or not?"

"You ought to go on home, cowboy," Morgan said.

"The hell. I'm alright. I don't have to work for two days. And I sure as hell don't need no cotton-spined no account to tell me what to do."

Morgan burned a little hotter, but he tried to keep his face flat and expressionless. His eyes bored into Slayton's, pinning the man's gaze like a captured butterfly and forcing him to struggle to break it free. Slayton was frightened of something in Atwater, something that had insinuated itself invisibly across the narrow gulf between them. He felt a sudden chill, as if someone had opened a hidden door and let in a winter wind.

Slayton rubbed the tip of his tongue across his lips, but it was as dry as they were, and the raspy sound was like that of a shed rattler skin skittering across a sandy floor ahead of a stiff breeze. Morgan thought that might be exactly what it was.

"Alright," he said, "I'll buy you a drink. On one condition."

"What's that?"

"That you drink up and go home. Sleep it off."

"I don't need to go nowhere. I'm fine. And I don't need no sissy to tell me nothing."

Morgan could feel something in his gut churning a little more every time Slayton opened his mouth. He was trying to give the dumb bastard a way out, but Slayton was too drunk, or too stupid, to see it.

"I said I'd buy you a drink. You don't want it, fine by me. Just leave me alone."

Slayton shook his head. He appealed to the crowd with a look of diminished expectations sadly fulfilled. "Man's got no backbone. Got a string of cotton where his backbone ought to be." He reached behind his back and thumped his own spine with his knuckles. "Nothing there," he said, a lopsided grin sliding down one side of his face. "Nothing!"

"Buy your own damn drink, then. I have had a belly full of you," Morgan said. He stood up and kicked the chair away from his legs, then backed away from the table a step.

He stepped around the table and slipped alongside Slayton. The cowboy turned and tried to grab Morgan's shirtfront, but Morgan was too quick for him. He snaked out an arm and grabbed a fistful of biceps, digging in his fingers and squeezing hard as Slayton tried to pull away. "Listen to me, you dumb sonofabitch!"

Slayton turned a drunken, bleary-eyed face over his shoulder. His breath stank of whiskey, and under the smell of the booze there was the stench of bile, as if Slayton were about to bring up the contents of his stomach. Morgan wondered how the man had managed to get so drunk so quickly, but he had managed. And he was perilously close to paying a very high price for his accomplishment.

Slayton almost jerked free and Morgan brought his other hand up and latched onto Slayton's head. He forced the cowboy to turn toward Kinkaid. "You see the man in the black coat, Deak? That man wants to kill you. You understand? And he *will* kill you if you give him the least excuse. Now, if you want to stay alive, if you want to live long enough to go back to work on Monday, then you listen to me and get the hell out of here."

He let Slayton go, and the cowboy staggered a couple of steps before turning back to Morgan. "You sonofabitch," he shouted. "I don't have to take that from nobody." He bulled forward, his drunken legs wobbling beneath him, and Morgan caught him in the gut with a quick combination.

Slayton struggled to get up. Morgan, wanting to be rid of Slayton and put an end to the confrontation, took a couple of steps back. Deak balanced on the balls of his palms and on his toes, the natural bridge of his arched body presenting a tempting target. Brett Kinkaid, not one to resist such a temptation without good reason, swung the pointed toe of one of his fancy Mexican boots and caught Slayton in the pit of the stomach.

Slayton went down like a felled ox, spewing vomit in a wide arc as he rolled over on his back. The awful mess stank to high heavens. Kinkaid dropped into a crouch, yanked a scented handkerchief from his pocket, and held it to his nose and mouth.

Grabbing Slayton carefully, to avoid the smeared vomit on the cowhand's shirt, the marshal dragged him halfway to his feet. "You hear what the man said? He said I would kill you if you weren't careful. And the man wasn't lying, I *will* kill you. You should understand that. This town has had about enough of your crap. We don't need your kind around here. Now, get *up*!"

Kinkaid's voice was rising to a near hysterical pitch. He had just about lost control of himself. There was some crazed energy in his screaming, and Morgan knew it wouldn't take much for Kinkaid to plummet over the edge.

The marshal screamed again. "Get *up*! You worthless piece of shit, I said get *up*!"

Slayton seemed to be on the edge of understanding just how dangerous his situation was, and he tried again to get to his feet, but his hands kept slipping in his vomit, and he fell to the floor each time he tried to rise. He was getting desperate, and got his body arched again. As he turned to avoid slipping, his pistol slipped out of his holster and landed in the puddled mess. He looked at it, then at Kinkaid. His eyes speared past the marshal for an instant toward Morgan, a look of uncomprehending desperation glazing them over the way oil will slick the surface of a pond.

He reached for the gun and Morgan saw Kinkaid tense. Slayton was about to hand the marshal the excuse he was looking for. Kinkaid's fingers curled, then relaxed as he went for his gun. Morgan leapt forward, his hand grabbing Kinkaid's right wrist and pinning it to his hip.

"Let it go, Kinkaid. He was just trying to pick up the damn gun. You know that. You had no call to pull down on him."

"Mind your own goddamned business, cowboy."

Morgan ignored him. "Somebody get Slayton out of here. Take him someplace. I don't care where, just take him the hell out of here."

Riley Grand was in the crowd, and he stepped forward to grab Slayton by one arm and haul him to his feet. Once up, the cowhand tried to break away, but Grand held on and he called to another hand from the outfit. The second man grabbed Slayton's other arm. Together, they started to drag him away. But Slayton, as if he didn't realize Atwater had just saved his life, shouted, "You bastard." He struggled with his friends and screamed again, his neck taut, the tendons bulging like steel bands stretched to the breaking point. "You bastard."

They hauled him outside. When the double doors finally stopped swinging, Morgan could still hear Slayton shouting as they dragged him down the street. Morgan let go of the marshal, who whirled on him. The marshal's face was contorted into something beyond human. It reminded Morgan of pictures he'd seen in a book, some monstrous creatures high along the roof of a French church. It was that grotesque.

"You shouldn't have done that, cowboy. You don't understand what the hell is going on here."

"The hell I don't."

"You were interfering with a peace officer in the act of performing his duty."

"Bullshit. You like throwing your weight around. I understand that, alright. You feel like you have to prove something to somebody. Yourself, most likely. I understand that, too. Better than you think. But there was no call to go after that man. None. And everybody in this goddamned bar knows it."

"The man's right, Marshal," somebody in the crowd shouted. "Deak don't mean nothing. That's just the way he is."

"You stupid bastards," Kinkaid shouted. "Slayton's gonna kill somebody one of these days. You ought to think about that."

"So you stop that by killing him first, Marshal? Is that how it is?" It was someone else in the crowd this time, and Kinkaid scanned their faces one by one, daring the speaker to step forward. But no one moved.

They were all the same, he thought. They hire somebody, a man like Brett Kinkaid, to do their dirty work. Then, when he does just what they pay him to do, they turn on him. That's the way it always was.

But not this time, he thought. Not this one goddamned time. He turned on Morgan. "You watch your step, mister. You see me coming, you tippy toe. You see what I'm saying? Tippy toe."

CHAPTER 4

Morgan Atwater was at the livery stable before the sun had cleared the horizon. The old man who ran the place was already there, slogging out the stalls. He worked with a beat-up old broom that had more handle than straws, and it scraped at the hard-packed dirt as he shoved mounds of damp straw toward the back door.

Without missing a stroke of the poor excuse for a broom, he said, "Up early, ain't you, stranger?"

"Got some business to attend to."

"I just bet you do."

"What's that supposed to mean?"

"It means you been buffaloed by Brett Kinkaid, same as most folks around here."

"You mean the marshal?"

"Could be I do. Then again, maybe you know

another Brett Kinkaid in town. Course, I've only been here twenty-six years next month. Could be I don't know as many folks around these parts as you do. Could be that."

"What's so special about Kinkaid?"

"To me, nothin'." He shrugged, then leaned on the broom. "But to some folks, a man with a blur where his right hand's supposed to be seems like manna from heaven. Me, I ain't impressed."

"You saying Kinkaid's a gunfighter?"

"Not me. That's what other folks are saying. Me, I'm saying nothing. Unless you ask."

"I'm asking," Atwater said.

"Well, then, since you asked, I'm saying he's a bully, sure enough. I seen his kind before. Hide behind a gun, throw a little weight around. And if a pack of damn fools wants to pin a badge on you and pay you to boot, well, hell, why not?"

"I don't think I'd go that far, Mr. Milton."

"No. You're a younger man than I am. You got more life ahead of you than I got behind me. I can afford to speak my mind, in the right company."

"Why didn't you say something before Kinkaid was hired?"

"Don't think I didn't, cowboy. I talked a blue streak to these iron heads. Not a one of 'em wanted to listen. I seen it before, and I guess I'll live to see this one play out, too. No reason to make me a notch on no gun butt. Kinkaid ain't likely to come lookin' for me, now, is he?"

Atwater shook his head. "You sayin' he'll come looking for me?"

"Look, I was there last night. I saw what happened. Lot of folks, me included, know you done the right thing. They think it took uncommon gumption to do it, too. Know it did. But I seen the look on Kinkaid's face. Hatred as pure as anything I ever seen. Plain as day, too. He ain't gonna forget you made him look the fool."

"You think I ought to worry about him, is that it? Maybe back-shooting?"

"I don't know you. Don't know him, neither, for all of that. But he ain't above that sort of thing. It don't take a prognosticator to see that. It's in his face. But I don't know for sure what he'll do. All I'm saying is he'll look to make a little bigger name for hisself. He can have his pick of these grass green cowpokes. They're always half liquored up anyhow, so it's like shootin' fish in a barrel. You ever done that?"

"Done what, get liquored up?"

"Nope. Don't have to ask that. You got a few hogsheads under your belt, I reckon. Shoot fish in a barrel. You ever done that?"

"No, I can't say as I have."

"You might try it sometime. Then you'll have some idea of what I'm talking about. You want your horse, I suppose?"

"If it's no trouble."

"What if it was trouble?"

"Then I guess I'd come back when it wouldn't be."

Milton laughed. "You're just too damn easygoin' to be believed."

"I wouldn't bank on that, old-timer."

Milton looked him hard in the face. The old

man's eyes seemed to grow bigger in the early morning light as he leaned toward Atwater. Finally, he shrugged. "No, I don't think I would. Give me five minutes. You can have your horse then. Wait in the office over there." He cocked his head over one shoulder toward a tiny cubicle near the front door.

Atwater nodded, walked to the small room, and stepped inside. It featured a small table, one of its four legs balanced on a slab of wood to keep it from wobbling too much, and two ladderback chairs with the slats missing.

As Atwater lowered himself into the chair in front of the desk, it creaked alarmingly, swayed until he braced himself with one foot, then the whole precarious assembly settled down with a final groan.

Milton was as good as his word. Five minutes later he was standing in the office doorway. Atwater hadn't even heard him approach. When he became aware of the old man's gaze, he turned to see Milton looking at him oddly, his head tilted at an angle, like that of a curious bird.

"You do favor somebody I seen once," Milton said. "I can't put a finger on it, but I know I seen you before. Never been through here, have you?"

"Nope."

"It'll come to me. In the meantime, though, I'd steer clear of Marshal Kinkaid. You look to me like the kind of man he likes to memorialize with a notch. Maybe even two."

"Tell me about Kinkaid."

"Tell you what?"

"Whatever you know."

"Ain't much to tell. Cross Creek was gettin' to be a hellhole. All them hands comin' in and kickin' up their heels of a payday. Got so ordinary folks didn't much want to come in town, much. Ain't good for business. Somebody, I think it was Tate Crimmins, heard Kinkaid was lookin' for work. He handled it pretty much by hisself."

"What do you mean, looking for work?"

"I mean the same thing anybody means. He was out of a job. Course, Tate didn't much care why. He knew Kinkaid was quick, and that he didn't mind a little mess. That was his stock in trade, anyhow, accordin' to Tate. Supposed to have cleaned up three, four other towns. Someplace in Kansas. He was down in Colorado, last. Got hisself run out of a job, though. Too quick, some people said. Hair trigger. And when there wasn't no trouble, he went around lookin' to see could he scare some up. Least, that's the way I heard it."

"You tell Crimmins that?"

"Hell, I told ever'body'd listen. Only nobody would. See, I do a good business on weekends. A lot of them hands board their mounts with me. The way Tate was lookin' at it, I didn't want a strong marshal 'cause it would scare them hands off. That it would hurt my business. Tate's wrong, though. Hands still got to drink, and they still got to leave their mounts someplace. Wasn't gonna make no difference to me."

Atwater leaned back in the rickety chair. The old man tensed for a second, as if waiting for the chair to collapse, but Atwater was careful.

"Wish I could remember where I seen you

before, though. Surely have. I know that much."

"It'll come to you."

"What'd you say your name was?"

"I didn't."

"Ashamed of it?" Milton asked.

Atwater chewed at his lower lip. He took a long time answering, and when he did, he surprised both himself and Milton. "Of my name, no. Of my past, yeah, I reckon I am."

"Uncommon honesty, Mr. . . ."

The blank hung in the air. Atwater declined to fill it, and Milton shrugged.

"What brings you to these parts?"

"Looking for someone. A woman, name of Kate Atwater. At least, that used to be her name. Now, I don't know."

"You come to the right place. I know Katie. You kin?"

"Not exactly."

Milton shook his head, as if trying to dislodge something. "I can tell you how to get to her place. Nice little spread, up in the Laramie foothills. About a ten-mile ride, maybe twelve. I . . ." He stopped suddenly. The gnarled fingers snapped without a sound, except for the wrinkled, parchment-like skin of Milton's right hand. "Atwater! That's where I seen you before. In the newspapers. That's your name, ain't it? Morgan Atwater. I'll be damned." The old man cackled, and Atwater was wondering whether it was because the old man jogged his memory loose or for some other reason.

The liveryman's next words made it clear. "You best steer clear of Marshal Kinkaid, then. You surely should. He knows who you are, he's damn sure gonna look to git his own ugly face in the papers. Course, it'll just be a bad likeness. The paper here don't do nothing fancy, except them pencil drawings. Not like them big city papers. But he'd like to see his name in big letters. I know that. You could be just the ticket he needs, if you see what I mean."

"Not if you don't tell him who I am."

"Who, me? Shoot, I don't tell him the time of day if he asks. I ain't gonna tell him who you are. But somebody else will figure it out, you stay around long enough. And when they do, they will not be backward about sharing the news with some more of the empty heads live in this damn fool town. And, sooner or later, Kinkaid will know. When he does, you better be ready. The longer you stay, the more likely it is. You *are* gonna stay awhile, ain't you?"

"I don't know."

"You Katie's brother?"

Atwater shook his head. Milton didn't take the hint though. Again, he snapped his ancient fingers. "That must be your boy. He does kinda favor you. Maybe that's where I seen your face. On Katie's boy."

Atwater stood up. "Look, Mr. Milton, I didn't come here for trouble. I'd appreciate it if you'd keep this between us."

"Don't worry about that. I won't say nothing to nobody. You want to know how to get to Katie's, I reckon I can point you right enough. Come on."

Atwater followed him into the barn. Milton tugged the bay along in his wake, then on out the back door. Once outside, he handed the reins to

Morgan. He climbed into the saddle and looked down at the old man, who looked rather solemn.

"You go on up the creek bottom about three miles. You come to a branch, and you follow it off to the left. Katie's three valleys over. Lazy M, she calls it. You can't miss it. There ain't no road, but you'll find it. The west fork runs right across her spread."

"Thank you."

"You comin' back tonight?"

"I expect. Why?"

"You and Katie ain't seen each other in a spell. I figger you got a lot to talk about. You know what I mean?" He chuckled. Then, to make certain Atwater didn't miss his meaning, he added, "That Katie's a mighty fine-lookin' woman. Even now."

"It's not like that," Atwater said.

"Maybe," Milton answered. He was still chuckling when he disappeared back into the stable.

CHAPTER 5

Morgan Atwater sat on his horse for a long time, staring down at the small ranch below him. The place was neat and well cared for, almost perfect. It had a view of the Laramies behind it, lush grass for the livestock, and plenty of clear, cold water. It looked like the place he had dreamed of so many years ago, still slopping hogs on his father's farm in Illinois. When he had left, it was nothing but a rude house in the wilderness, a small corral, and a shed. Now it was a real ranch. Katie's ranch.

All the way up from Texas, he had tried to imagine what it would look like. Now he was looking at it, and he couldn't believe it. He climbed down from his horse and curled the reins in his hand. Dropping to the ground, he leaned back and watched the clouds overhead. They were so high up, almost as distant as that dream and the time in which he dreamed it. So much had happened since then.

Part of him wanted to mount up and ride away, to leave the dream behind. The urge to bolt was so powerful, he was afraid to get up, for fear he would act on it. Watching the clouds did little to calm him. He could hear his heart thumping in his chest, a huge, distant drum. It seemed like the ground beneath him vibrated with every beat, rattling his bones and threatening to tear them joint from joint.

He closed his eyes for a moment, and when he reopened them, a solitary hawk sailed across the sky, its great wings beating twice as it found an air current and started to climb. Then, spotting something, it tucked its wings and fell like a stone. Atwater sat up to watch as the bird plummeted, fanning its wings at the last moment, still falling, talons extended. There was a brief flutter of the great wings, then they settled into a steady stroke as the bird began to climb. Atwater watched the struggle of a small rabbit for a few seconds, then turned away.

It was the order of things, the way of the world, really, but he didn't want to watch. When he turned back, the hawk was a small speck far across the valley. He sighed and got to his feet. Keeping a tight grip on the reins, he started to walk downhill. At first, every step was slow, deliberate. He was stalling and he knew it. But he didn't know any other way to do what he had to do.

When the land bottomed out, he felt more in control of himself. He steeled into a steady gait, the horse matching him stride for stride, barely tugging on the reins. He angled across the meadow studded with Indian paintbrush and columbine. Bees swarmed around him, diving in toward his face, and he batted them away with his free hand. He was grinning, and it made him feel foolish, but the place was so pretty, he couldn't help himself, and wouldn't if he could.

The tall grass was lush and green, and the fragrance of the blades crushed under his boots swirled in the air around him. At first, he wondered if anyone else felt this way, surrounded by so much beauty and so much vibrant life. Then, realizing how selfish he was being, he wondered that not everyone did feel that way. It was what life was supposed to be, what he had dreamed it could be, before he grew up. Before he knew better. And he was amazed that something deep inside him could still respond so powerfully to something so simple.

And other memories kept crowding in on him. He remembered back before his son was born, they had just finished the first house. Katie wanted a bath, to celebrate, she said. It was near nightfall, but it was warm, and he had filled a huge cauldron with water from the creek. Then he added a half-dozen pails of hot water heated one by one over the fire.

He could still see her now, her skin picking up a metallic tint from the sun as it began to set. Her body was perfect, so much softer than the other women he had known, but stronger, too, as if she had bones of steel. And the curves were right where they were supposed to be.

Standing there naked, her red hair almost a cloak all the way down to the backs of her thighs, turned, one leg bent at the knee as she stepped into the bath, she looked like a golden statue. That moment had frozen in time somehow. It was how he always saw her, all golden and round . . . and perfect. It was how he still saw her.

Morgan moved toward a broad, shallow stream, stepped in, and, instead of crossing, decided to follow it a way. The water wet his cuffs, but he didn't care. It was so clear it hurt his eyes to look at the reflected sunlight and the fine white quartz sand glittering under the ripples kicked up by an occasional rock. He could see the front of the house, and a small curl of smoke suddenly puffed up through the chimney. It was almost eight o'clock now, probably breakfast being made, maybe a pot of coffee. Katie had always made good coffee.

The front door opened as he reached a small, raw timber bridge over the creek, and he climbed up the shallow bank and onto the dirt road. A figure appeared on the front porch, but he was too far away to recognize it. Whoever it was noticed him. The figure curled a hand over its eyes and leaned toward him. A moment later the door opened again and the figure vanished inside, only to reappear with a carbine in hand.

He started to walk a little faster now, tugging on the reins to get the horse to move. When he reached a gate in the split rail fence, he slowed again. The figure stepped off the porch. He could tell now that it was a woman.

The woman moved gracefully, but cautiously. Not walking, exactly, but not running either. The carbine was cradled across her arms, comfortably, even naturally, the way a woman carries an infant. There was no longer any doubt in his mind. It was Kate.

She seemed to sense something and stopped in her tracks. She leaned back on her heels, the carbine, he could tell it was a Winchester now, crooked in one elbow.

She looked at him for a long time without speaking. He slowed a bit, then stopped altogether. He took off his hat and ran one hand through his hair.

"Is it you, then?" she asked.

"Hello, Katie."

"It's been a long time," she said. It wasn't bitter, just sort of distant, the way you might say it to someone you had known in school and not particularly liked.

"Fifteen years."

"That long?"

Atwater nodded. "That long."

"What do you want?"

Atwater heaved a sigh. He shifted his feet, unable to get comfortable. He glanced down at them as if to reprimand them, and for the first time realized he had gotten wet. "I thought I ought to set a few things in order. It seemed like time, I guess."

She nodded. Her free hand went to her cheek, fussed with a few strands of red hair, then fell to her side. "You want some coffee?"

"You still put egg shells in it?"

"Yes, I do."

"Then I'd like a cup, if it's no trouble."

"I've had trouble from you all my life, Morgan.

A cup of coffee is nothing at all, compared to that."

"We'll talk about it," he said.

"Not likely," she said, turning on her heel and heading back toward the house. She moved quickly now, gradually widening the distance between them until she stood on the porch. Then she turned and nodded her head toward the corral. "You can put your horse in there, if you want," she said.

Her cheeks were glistening, but he didn't realize it was from tears until she reached up to wipe them away. "I'm sorry if I upset you," he said. "I mean, showing up this way."

She nodded. "Come on inside. Clean your boots first, though."

He laughed, and she gave him a look. Then she laughed, too. "You're right. Some things don't ever change."

It looked the way he expected it to look. Everything was in its place. In Katie Atwater's world, if something didn't have a place, it didn't belong at all. A small fire crackled in the fireplace, a black iron coffeepot suspended over it from a hook.

Morgan sat down at a rough but sturdy table. The tablecloth was spotless and showed not a single wrinkle.

"It looks better than I remember," he said.

Kate turned to him from a cabinet, a pair of thick mugs in her hands, "It *is* better than you remember," she said. Then, setting the mugs on the table, she backed away a step. "Sorry, I didn't mean that the way it sounded."

"Yes, you did. But it's alright. You're entitled. You don't owe me any apologies."

She laughed again. "Is that what I was doing? Apologizing? God knows, I didn't mean to."

"How's the boy?"

"You remember what this place looked like but you don't remember his name? Is that it?"

Morgan shook his head. "Of course not. It's just that I . . . well, it seemed too personal. I don't have . . ." He let his hands flutter helplessly.

"Too personal? He's your son, for God's sake. Too personal? You don't remember his name, do you?"

It was a challenge, and something welled up inside of him. He wasn't going to knuckle under. Not this time. "Yes, I do."

"Then what is it? Tell me. Use it, for Christ's sake."

"I don't remember you cussing like that."

"You don't know me at all, Morgan Atwater. Don't you be telling me what I am or what I was or what you think I should be. Just don't you dare."

"I wouldn't. I don't have the right. I know that."

"The right? Is that what this is all about? Do you have the right to show up here after fifteen years? Do you have that right? Do you? Answer me, dammit!" She turned away from him.

"Sit down, Katie. Please."

Instead, she took the coffeepot and lugged it to the table. She used a thick handmade potholder in either hand. When she poured the coffee, he noticed that her hands were trembling. A small spot of coffee splashed on the tablecloth, quickly spread out, and she slammed the pot down.

Katie covered her face with her hands. The hot

pot scorched the tablecloth, filling the room with the smell of burnt cotton. Morgan pushed his chair back, got up, and retrieved the pot. He hung it back over the fire. She still hadn't said anything, and he couldn't bring himself to look at her. But he knew she was watching him now. He shifted the mugs and the small sugar bowl, rolled the scorched cloth into a neat cylinder, and turned to her.

"What do you want me to do with this?"

"Take it and get out. That's what I want you to do. But you won't." She glared at him. "Will you?"

"Not till I've done what I came for."

"And what might that be?"

"I got a lot to make up to you and the boy."

"Stop calling him that. He has a name. Why don't you use it?"

Atwater took a sip of his coffee. It was hot, but he didn't react. He set the mug down again. And got to his feet. "Maybe you're right. Maybe I shouldn't have come here."

"Morgan, wait. You're here now, stay."

Atwater turned. Kate was moving toward the table. She sat down, never taking her eyes off him. "You sure?" he asked.

She nodded. "It's just . . . it's been . . ."

"I know," he said.

He sat down again. "Where's Tommy?"

"It's Tom," she said. "He outgrew Tommy a long time ago."

CHAPTER 6

Deak Slayton woke up with a bad headache. He didn't remember much about the night before, but he knew he had been angry about something. It kept pricking at the back of his skull, and he lay there in the hotel room trying to get it in focus. He glanced over at the woman next to him. He didn't remember meeting her, and wasn't sure of her name. He remembered it was French, or sounded French, anyway. Fifi, Lola, something like that, he thought it was.

He sat up slowly, lowered his feet to the floor, and tensed his shoulders. His head felt like it was about to fall off, or as if it had already fallen off and someone had done him the dubious favor of nailing it back on.

He walked to the window, aware that his long-johns smelled worse than usual. He glanced at Fifi, but she was still sound asleep. He knew she wasn't faking because she was snoring like a mad bull. He pulled the curtain aside and the sudden explosion of harsh sunlight melted his eyeballs. In the brilliant wash of illumination, Lola looked about as good as she sounded.

Deak pulled on his jeans and his boots, slipped into his spare shirt, and strapped on his gunbelt, trying to make as little noise as possible. He didn't remember whether he had paid for the room, but the clerk would let him know on the way out. He didn't have any doubt about that.

He was halfway down the hall when he remembered he hadn't left anything for the woman. He started back, then shrugged. He could always pay her later, if she remembered what he owed. What he needed was a little hair of the dog. Hell, it was Saturday, and he had the whole damn day to feel good. Why did his head have to hurt so much?

Deak clapped his hat on as he stepped into the lobby. He glanced at the clerk, who paid no attention to him, and he assumed he had paid. As he pushed open the double glass doors, he winced as the sunlight slammed him in the face. It was already past ten o'clock, and his mouth felt like the underside of a saddle. The sooner he got something to kill his thirst, the sooner he'd start feeling better. At least that's what he told himself as he squinted across the street.

Largo's Saloon was already open. It wouldn't be long. He remembered being mad at Riley Grand, too, but he couldn't remember why. Hell, he was always getting mad at Riley. The bastard talked too much and said too little. It was getting to be a bit too boring around Cross Creek. It just might be time to move on. He could head on up to Montana, even thought he might, once or twice.

Another month, and he'd have enough money, if he left as soon as he got paid. That had always been the hard part. But hell, he was a grown man. He didn't have to spend his money if he didn't want to. He could just pocket his pay, maybe even a week early, to avoid the temptation, and head on up to Butte, or someplace. His cousin was up there somewhere. Deak had had a card from him, if he could just remember where...

Largo's was quiet when he walked in. Pete Largo was behind the bar, mopping up lamplight with a wet rag. The owner glanced at him once, wrinkled his face in something that was either a frown or a smile, and took a couple more swipes with the rag.

"Morning, Pete," Slayton said. His voice was too loud, and it made his temples throb. He tried again, this time softer. "How you doin'?"

"Deak."

"Can I get a beer?"

"Can you pay for it, or did you drop it all on Monique?"

"Monique, is that her name?"

"It is this week."

Slayton laughed. Largo didn't. The barman turned away and walked down the bar, swiping at a full-length mirror with his cloth. It left swirls of sparkling moisture on the glass, but he didn't seem to mind. Grabbing a heavy-bottomed mug, he moved to the tap at the far end of the bar, jerked it open, and filled the mug.

He set the glass on the bar and gave it a shove. It slid along the damp wood, until it hit a sticky spot. It lost some momentum, and a small tidal wave of beer and foam sloshed on ahead. When the mug pulled out of the sticky place, it hit the beer-slickened wood and picked up speed again.

Deak grabbed for it, but missed. The mug slid on to the curve at the end of the bar, made it halfway around, then ran out of steam. Slayton laughed. "You losing your touch, Pete, or am I?"

"I ain't losing nothing but money, Deak."

"I know how that is."

"You know how it is around here, do you?"

"What do you mean?"

"You know damn well what I mean, Deak. I mean the marshal. He's got it in for you. Hell, he's got it in for half the town, seems like."

"He's a hard case. So what? I've seen guys like him before. They blow into some little town, throw their weight around, then blow on out a couple months later. It's no big deal. Besides, I'm thinking of going to Montana." He drank half the beer in one long swallow.

"Maybe you ought to stop thinking about it, and just do it."

"You think I'm scared of him?" He sipped more slowly now.

"I think you should be. Deak, I'm telling you, the man is pure poison. You don't know the half of it."

"I know enough. But what the hell, Pete. It just

adds a little spice, you know? Like some damn leathery stew a mess cook'll throw together when he's running out of everything but flour and beans. What's he do? He throws some spices in, covers up a lot of sins that way. Life's like that. A little spice never hurt nothing. Not me, anyhow."

"This could do more than hurt you. This guy's got a mean streak in him a yard wide, Deak. I don't know you very well, but you've always been straight with me. You pay your tab, and you don't make no more trouble than you have to, I guess. I don't want to see nothing happen to you. That's all I'm saying."

"I appreciate it, Pete. Truly. But I let this guy run me out of town, I can't never shave again, because I wouldn't be able to look at myself in the mirror. Can you imagine me with whiskers? Well, can you?"

"That would sure enough be an awful sight, Deak."

"There you go. See, I got to stay." He downed the last of his drink and slid the mug across the bar. "Give me another beer, would you?"

In silence, Slayton finished his second beer and started on a third while Largo went into the back to check his stock. He tried to keep up a running conversation, but Deak couldn't hear him very well, and it hurt his head to shout, so he said good-bye and drifted on out of the saloon.

The sun was full out, and it was getting hot, hotter than it should be, almost, for the time of year. Wyoming wasn't supposed to feel like Texas, even in late July. But it did. Deak was working up a half decent sweat as he walked up the street.

When he got to The Hangin' Tree, he debated going in, decided not, until he spotted Kinkaid through the open door of the marshal's office. He shrugged and changed course. Climbing onto the boardwalk, he dropped into a chair and leaned back against the wall. He could hear the piano tinkling inside and pulled his pocket watch out. It was almost noon, kind of early for the buzzing in his ears. He wondered if he had managed to sleep off the night's drinking after all. Three beers shouldn't have been enough to make his ears ring like that.

After a couple of minutes, Kinkaid appeared in the door of his office. He leaned against the door frame. He wasn't wearing a jacket today, and Deak noticed how Kinkaid's gun sat easy on his hip, just out of reach of his fingertips. There was something about the marshal made him feel just a bit uncomfortable.

In the back of his mind, the truth kept gnawing at him. What it was, was Pete Largo was right. Kinkaid did have it in for him, and he knew it. He didn't know why, but that scarcely mattered. No man worth his salt would let himself be cowed, even by a man with a badge. Maybe this was the time to let Kinkaid know it. He thought about it for a long time, the marshal just leaning there in the doorway, staring at him.

It was unnerving, and Deak didn't have the stomach for that kind of thing so early. He didn't mind a good brawl, but bare knuckles was one thing and going toe to toe with a trigger-happy badge was something else again.

Rather than withstand the pressure of those flat,

black, and unblinking eyes, Deak got up and went inside. He didn't look back over his shoulder, even after the door closed behind him, but he knew the marshal was grinning. And that just made him mad.

He ordered a whiskey from the bartender, then sat at a vacant table in the corner, nursing his drink and his anger. Part of him wanted to storm across the street and tell Kinkaid to leave him alone, and part of him wanted to climb on his horse and light out for Montana with nothing in his pocket.

Instead, he had another whiskey, then a third. The bartender was reluctant to serve him the last one. It was too early for somebody to have such red eyes and such slurred speech. But Deak Slayton had a bad temper, and everybody knew it. It was better just to let him have his own way, and stand back.

On the fourth whiskey, the bartender drew the line, bad temper or no. "You had enough, Deak," he said.

"You don't be telling me that, Johnny. I know when I had enough, not you."

"But Mr. Carlson told me not to even serve you. I give you three. You get in a ruckus, and it'll cost me my job."

"There won't be no ruckus if you bring me my whiskey."

"Can't do it, Mr. Slayton."

"The hell you can't." Deak grabbed the kid by the suspenders and jerked him over the bar. That was his first mistake. Johnny got up scared and broke for the door. He flew through it with his head down and tumbled into the street. The marshal saw

him and was halfway across the street by the time
Johnny was on his feet again.

"What's the trouble, son?" he asked.

"No trouble. I, unh, I just lost my balance, Marshal, that's all. Honest."

"Sure. Deak Slayton wouldn't happen to be the
reason you lost your balance, now, would he?"

"No, sir. Just careless, I guess. That's all."

"Where you headed?"

"No place. I just..."

A gunshot drowned out the next couple of
words, and breaking glass the rest of his answer.
The marshal patted him on the shoulder. "You just
wait here, son. I'll handle this."

"I can get Mr. Carlson. He'll take care of it."

"No he won't, son. I will."

Kinkaid was already on the boardwalk. He
stepped into the bar to find Deak Slayton drinking
from a broken bottle of bourbon. He had cut his
lip on the sharp edge, but didn't seem to have noticed.

"Better put that bottle down, Deak."

"Nah. It ain't empty." Slayton took another pull,
this time spilling whiskey all down the front of his
shirt.

"I said you better put it down."

Slayton set the bottle on the bar. He tried to
be careful, but it tipped over anyway and spilled
onto the floor with a loud splat. He gave a long sigh
of exasperation. "I guess we might as well get to
it," he said.

"Doesn't have to be like this, Deak."

"Sure it does, Marshal. You been wanting to

pull down on me since I come to town. What's the use of waiting any longer."

"Just put up your gun, real easy. Lay it on the bar, and that'll be the end of it."

"You know that ain't so, Marshal."

"Have it your way."

Slayton shook his head. "No, sir. We'll have it your way. That'll be just fine."

He wiggled his fingers to loosen them, then went for it. Kinkaid was a lot faster. He put one in Deak Slayton's chest, just above the third shirt button. Deak slid down the front of the bar, leaving a long, dark, shiny smear on the wood. In the dim lamplight, it looked almost like creosote.

Deak swallowed once, then a small bubble of blood ballooned between his lips. He groaned, the rush of air bursting the bubble. Then it got quiet.

CHAPTER 7

"**S**o," Morgan said. "The boy — Tommy — he's not here, then?"

"He'll be back. And it's Tom. I already told you that."

"Go easy on me, Katie. It's been a long time."

She laughed, a harsh, explosive sound that seemed to die as soon as it left her lips. "Oh, Morgan. You have a funny sense of time, you do. It's not been a long time, it's been a lifetime, Tom's lifetime. *My* lifetime, dammit. And in some ways it seems like yesterday. I can still see you on that black horse, riding away like you'd be back in an hour. Why, Morgan? Was I so bad? Was it so bad having a family, is that why you left?"

Atwater stared down at his hands crawling restlessly across the bare wood of the table. When he spoke, he didn't look up. "No, Katie, it wasn't so bad."

Kate barely heard him. He knew it, but he wasn't going to say it again unless she asked. As he knew she would. "I didn't hear that," she said.

"I said no. It wasn't that."

He looked up at her now, fearful of what he might see. He knew she hated him, and believed she was right to hate him. But he wanted her to understand. He had only just come to understand it himself, and he wasn't yet comfortable with the knowledge. Never very good at explaining things, he knew he had to try, because this was his one chance.

"I want to understand, you know. I think I have that right."

"You do. I don't know if I can...hell..."

"Talk to me, Morgan. I'm the mother of your son."

He took another sip of the coffee, already growing cold where it sat in the big mug. "Maybe that's why, Katie. Maybe I..."

She blew up then. "That's not why and you know it."

"Give me a chance. You want to know, and I want to tell you."

"You had fifteen years to rehearse, Morgan. I should think you'd have it all set by now."

He smashed a big fist on the table. "Damn it!" The mugs jumped an inch or so, and hers, untouched, sloshed coffee over its lip. The warm coffee lay there in a small dark pool, still steaming a little. They both watched the tiny coils of mist. "I never liked myself much, didn't like what I was turning into. I wanted to be something different, something you and the boy could be proud of. But that wasn't possible. Not then."

"You could have changed. You just didn't want to."

"They wouldn't let me."

"They. Who's they, Morgan? Who do you want to blame it on?"

"I blame myself, no one else. But it wasn't just me. You don't wake up one morning and say, 'It's a beautiful day. I think I'll pretend I never owned a gun.' You can't do that, Katie. I couldn't, anyway. Because there's always someone out there who won't let you forget. Sure, I could have stayed here. But one day, maybe in a week, maybe a month, somebody would have ridden up to the front door with one thing on his mind."

"Oh, you're a mind reader now, too, are you? You can read the minds of people you never even met. Read them before they even got here. Is that how it is?"

"I . . ."

He stopped when he heard a footstep on the porch. His hand was on his gun before he realized what he was doing. Kate saw it, and he saw that she did. She shook her head. "You haven't changed at all, have you?"

"Yes, I have."

"So, you think your own son is going to shoot you?"

Morgan was stunned. She had said the boy was coming back, but not when. He hadn't expected him so soon. He wasn't ready. His eyes darted to her face. He hoped she would understand and offer him something, some way out. Katie smiled a bitter smile.

"The gunfighter." There was such contempt in her voice he wondered that it didn't sear the flesh from her lips as she spoke. "I won't let you hide, I won't let you run away. Not this time. Not until you've done what you came for, whatever that is."

Atwater stood, but his knees were like liquid. He tottered and was worried she might think him drunk. She offered no help. When he started for the door, he glanced back at her, but she was still at the table, her hands folded on the rough wood. Her face was empty.

Chewing at his lower lip, he stepped all the way to the door, looked back again, and, when she hadn't moved, accepted that he was on his own. He opened the screen door, his hand shaking as he extended it, and again when he let it go as he passed through.

A brace of partridge tied by the feet lay on the porch, and a shotgun leaned against the wall.

He saw the boy then, not a boy really, but not quite a man yet, loosening the cinch on a big chestnut mare. Tom, he thought, I have to remember to call him Tom, not Tommy.

Tom hadn't heard him or, if he did, paid no attention. He finished removing the saddle, tucked it up on his shoulder, and lugged it to the stable. Morgan stood there poised above the top step of the porch, wondering whether he should go to meet the boy or stay where he was. As hostile as Kate had seemed, he felt somehow comforted knowing she was just a few feet away.

The boy appeared in the doorway and seemed to notice Morgan for the first time. He stopped, one foot suspended for a brief second. When it touched down, all movement ceased. The boy had become a statue. Morgan was amazed. Looking at the boy, even at that distance, he had the sensation of looking in an old mirror, seeing an image older even than the boy himself. They were spitting images.

Morgan tilted his head back and cocked it to one side. Tom did the same, screwing up his face to peer through the glare of the late morning sun. The similarity was overwhelming. Morgan had the sensation of watching himself as a young man. If only he had known then what he knew now.

Tom finally started to move. He walked slowly, his eyes still screwed tight, more in puzzlement now than an effort to see more sharply. Morgan was afraid to move. When Tom reached the bottom step, Morgan pushed his hat back so the boy could see him more easily.

"Something I can do for you, mister?" Tom asked.

"No." It was Katie who answered. The screen door squeaked as she pushed it open, and Morgan was aware of her stepping near him, not too close, but close enough.

Tom looked puzzled. "What's going on, Mom?"

"Why don't you ask him?" Kate said.

Tom looked more confused than ever now.

And he was getting angry. "Somebody better tell me what's going on, dammit."

Morgan twisted his head to loosen the knots at the base of his skull. "Maybe we better take a walk, son."

"What for?"

"Just bear with me."

"Go ahead, Tommy," Kate said. Morgan heard the diminutive and turned to look at her sharply. What was she trying to do, he wondered.

"Someplace you like, some special place, maybe, out there?" Morgan gestured vaguely with his hand.

Tom, still mystified, turned to look as if Morgan were indicating some particular place. He shrugged. "Not really," he said.

"Fine, then let's just walk." Not knowing what else to do, Morgan stepped down off the porch and headed across the yard. He was nearly to the gate before Tom caught up to him.

They walked side by side to the creek, and when Morgan stepped down off the bridge to the bank, Tom stopped. Morgan turned to see what was wrong.

"Why are we doing this?" Tom asked. "I know who you are."

"No you don't. You think you do, but what you know is what your mother wanted you to know. That's only one part of me."

"I can think for myself."

"But do you?"

"Damn right!"

Morgan nodded. "So why don't you tell me what you think, then?"

"You don't want to know."

"I'm askin', ain't I?"

"No. Not really. You came here to make yourself feel better, maybe. Maybe because you think you have some unfinished business. With me, or with Mom, maybe. But there's nothing you can do here. We learned to get along without you, because you left us no choice. Now that we learned, don't think we can ever go back, because we can't."

"That's not what I want, son."

"Don't call me that. I'm not your son. You're not my father. You were never a father to me. Hell, I look at you and I don't remember you at all. I don't have any memories, good or bad. If I could hate you for something I remembered, that would be different. But you never even gave me that. You're some stranger who rides in here like he has a right to be here. But you don't. I don't know what the hell you want, but it isn't here. You left me nothing, damn you. And there's nothing here for you, either. Nothing!"

"What I want is to tell you I'm sorry. To try to make it up to you and your mother somehow."

"Make it up to us?" Tom was incredulous. "Do you really think you can just snap your fingers and wipe away fifteen years? Well you can't. Now, if you have nothing else to say, it would be best if you left us alone. Again."

Morgan shook his head. "It's not that easy, Tom."

"It was before."

"That's not fair."

"Fair, is it? I don't have to be fair to you. I don't want to be fair to you. I don't give a damn about fair when it comes to you, and I don't think you even know the meaning of the word."

"But I do, you know. You think you know everything. That's only normal for a boy your age. But there's a lot more to being a man than knowing the answers. Sometimes, you got to stop and figure out the right questions. I don't think you've done that yet. Hell, I don't know if I've done it yet, either. But I got to try. And so do you."

"The hell I do."

"Damn it, Tom. Listen to me!"

"Why should I?"

Morgan took a deep breath, trying to calm his own anger and to get a grip on things. This wasn't how it was supposed to be. He hadn't expected it to be so hard.

"I could tell you what my father always used to say."

"What's that?"

"'Because I said so.' But that doesn't cut any ice with you. I know that. It never did with me, either. But I pretended it made a difference. I figured he'd earned the right to that much, at least. But I *didn't* earn the right. That's why I'm asking you, not telling you. If you're half the man you think you are, you'll at least give me that much."

Tom nodded. He was breathing hard, the anger still boiling in his gut, but he nodded again and lowered himself to the bridge. He let his feet dangle over the edge, and the water broke into little sprays where the surface grazed his heels. Morgan saw two little rainbows for a moment, where the fine spray scattered the sunlight.

"Alright."

CHAPTER 8

The ride back to Cross Creek was the longest of Morgan Atwater's life. He kept turning the situation over and over in his head. Each time, it started the same way. It had looked so promising. Kate had seemed, if not glad to see him, at least pleased that he was alive. Even that was more than he had allowed himself to hope for.

But it went sour so quickly. He wasn't surprised at that, not really. But he thought there must have been a way to handle it, some way that would have let him control the conversation, something he might have said that would have bought him some time. So he replayed the conversation over and over. He was like an obsessed playwright endlessly reworking a scene that had gone wrong. It wrecked the play, brought down the curtain at the end of the first act, leaving the remaining four stillborn. Dead promises, flowers never allowed to bloom.

It was his fault. He knew that, just as the playwright knows where the fault lies. But he didn't know how to do it right. He had broken a life, two lives, three, and there was no way to fix them. Two had mended on their own, like badly set bones. The leg would never again move as it was meant to, the arm never quite bend the way God had intended, but they worked. His own fracture, though, had never set at all. He could hear the scraping of unknit splinters of bone with every gesture. His was a life that had been so completely shattered that it could never be set right.

That was the one incontrovertible fact that he had overlooked. Now, Katie's home, the one he had hoped to build with his own hands so long ago, receding behind him as he rode over the crest of the first hill, he realized that nothing could ever undo what he had done. He didn't want to accept it, refused to accept it, but he knew it was true.

Still, he kept telling himself, there must be some atonement, some way to make things better than they had been. He had not allowed himself to expect anything, thinking only that he owed a debt that he was finally willing and able to pay. But it hadn't worked out that way. Thinking merely to soothe an old wound, he had succeeded only in reopening it.

But maybe that was a good thing, he thought. Maybe he had let out a little poison. Maybe there was still reason to hope. All he really wanted now was to go somewhere and stand up to his waist in cold, clear water and pull out a trout, a big, arching rainbow, and flip it onto the sand. With his son by his side. And Katie to sit down with the two of them to pick the flame-whitened flesh from the delicate bones. It wasn't much to ask.

Or was it?

The town wasn't much, either, but he'd be damned if he would leave. He wasn't the kind of man to give up so easily. If Morgan Atwater had learned one thing from his father, it was that a man owed something to his son. And that, whether the son wanted it or not, he had to give it to him.

He would find some way to make it work, just long enough for that simple meal, maybe, but he would have that. He could close his eyes then and let them cover him over. It would be alright. He would have done the one thing in his life that remained undone.

As Cross Creek suddenly loomed up in front of him, he slowed his horse, wondering if there was some way he could justify staying on. Maybe a week or so. If it took longer than that, then he'd be willing to admit it would never happen at all. But he'd give it that much time, anyway.

John Milton was sitting on a chair at the front of the livery stable as Atwater rode up. The old man stared at him as if he'd never seen him before. Atwater slid from the saddle and offered the reins to Milton. The old man snatched at them, but never left his chair.

"Marshal was looking for you," he said.

"What'd he want?"

"Didn't say."

"He want me to come by?"

"Don't know."

"You aren't so damn talkative, today, are you?"

"Nothin' to say."

Atwater nodded. He turned toward the hotel. Milton called after him, "Still staying the month?"

Atwater said nothing. He realized he didn't know how to answer the question. At the moment, all he could think about was Brett Kinkaid. He hadn't liked the man since he first laid eyes on him. Nothing he had seen or heard was calculated to change that initial impression.

The walk down the center of town seemed endless. He had the feeling that dozens of pairs of eyes followed him from behind curtains and under the bottom edge of lowered shades. He knew it was foolish, but the feeling wouldn't leave him.

He went straight to Kinkaid's office. The door was open, but no one was there. He sat in the lone chair across from Kinkaid's desk. He noticed the gun rack on the wall, a half-dozen long guns, mostly carbines and a single Sharps buffalo gun, were chained through the trigger guards and held by a heavy iron padlock. Kinkaid seemed to expect all-out war at any moment.

Atwater got up and looked in the back room. Three cells, their doors open, lined one wall. All three were empty. The other wall was cold, windowless stone. He sucked his teeth, and the sound echoed in the cell block three or four times, then faded away.

Moving back to the front office, he considered sitting down to wait. But there didn't seem to be anything he could gain. Instead, he rummaged through the desk's lone drawer, found the stub of a flat pencil, its lead rounded and worn almost to the wood. He scratched a short note, telling Kinkaid where he was staying and that he heard the marshal was looking for him. For a moment, he considered not signing it, then realized how foolish or egotistical or both it might look, and he scrawled his name. The point all but gave out as he neared the end of his last name, and the line he drew under it was just a leadless ditch in the rough paper.

Outside again, he stood on the boardwalk for a couple of minutes, thinking maybe Kinkaid would see him, but the street stayed as deserted as it had been on the way down from the stable. He had about a hundred dollars cash, and a letter of credit for one thousand dollars. That, and his horse and gun, were all he owned. But the thousand wasn't really his. That was for Tommy and Kate. If he wanted to stay on, he had better find a way to make some money. There wasn't much he couldn't do, and not much he hadn't done, but Cross Creek wasn't exactly the crossroads of the continent. He wondered if he could hire on with Deak Slayton's outfit, or one of the other spreads outside town.

Stepping into the street, he trudged back to the stable. Milton seemed to know everything that was happening in the town. If anybody was looking to hire, Milton would probably know about it. He found the old man right where he'd left him. The only difference was that he no longer had a fistful of the bay's reins.

"Back again, are you?" Milton asked.

"You know anybody needs a job of work done?"

"Couple or three people."

"You think I might trouble you for a recommendation?"

Milton seemed to mull it over. He hacked away at a willow twig with a tiny pocket knife. It looked as if he were trying to see just how thin he could slice the soft wood. His lap was full of inch-long curls, thin as rice paper and nearly transparent. Other than the accumulation of the shavings, the work seemed to have no earthly purpose.

"Check with Lyle Henessey, over to the general store. He needs a clerk. Unless that's not what you're looking for."

"I'm looking for anything that pays."

"Lyle don't pay much, but it's regular and the work ain't too hard on a man who's used to bending his back now and then. I reckon you are that, ain't you?"

Atwater nodded. "Thanks for the tip."

"I was you, though, I wouldn't bother."

"Why not?"

"The marshal figgers to run you off before you settle in."

"Is that a fact?"

"He knows who you are. And I ain't told him nothing. I don't know how he knows, but I know he does, 'cause he told me."

"Told you what?"

"I knew you was a shooter, but I didn't know how much of one. Kinkaid told me you kilt near a dozen men, the last one not six months ago. That right?"

"What do you think?"

"I think I asked you was that right."

"It's right."

"You fixin' to make the marshal your next one?"

"I don't kill men for fun, and I don't shoot everybody who deserves it."

"You sayin' shooting Kinkaid would be fun and that's why you won't do it?"

"You might say that."

Milton shook his head. "I wouldn't turn my back on the man, I was you. You know he shot Deak Slayton, don't you?"

"What?"

"Yessir. Shot him right through the chest. This mornin'. Right there in The Hanging Tree. Blood all over the damn bar. Pete seen it. He said it didn't have to happen, but Deak felt like he might as well get it over. And Kinkaid sure wasn't gonna let the chance pass."

"He just plain shot him, you say?"

"That's about right. Deak drinkin', as usual, and he run that youngster off was tending the bar. That's what brought Kinkaid flappin' them buzzard wings of his. Deak kind of pushed it, though, is what I hear. Like he wanted it to happen."

"What in the hell for?"

"Only Deak and the marshal know the answer to that one. The marshal won't say, an' Deak can't. Killed him, he did. Stone dead."

Atwater felt his blood thicken and for a moment

he wondered if his heart would beat again. He knew Kinkaid was a bad one, but this was worse than anything he had imagined. Last night, he figured Kinkaid would cool down, Slayton would sober up, and it would all blow away. But it hadn't. It had a life of its own, and Deak Slayton just got chewed up and spit out. But Milton wouldn't let him dwell on it. He said, "You ask me, I think the marshal's got you on his list, too."

Atwater nodded absently. He thanked Milton again for the lead, and walked on down the street to Henessey's General Store. Now he knew why he'd felt the eyes on his back. It hadn't been his imagination. They were all watching, waiting to see what was going to happen.

And he realized the worst was not really being sure himself.

Henessey was in. Atwater asked about the job, and Henessey hesitated. "I don't know if I can pay what you're looking for," he said.

"All I'm looking for is enough to keep body and soul together. I don't expect to get rich."

"Then you come to the right place. I can pay you eight dollars a week. If you can work for that, the job's yours. But there's two things I don't tolerate. One's drinking on the job. That's why I got a vacancy in the first place. And the other's lateness. You show up late just one time, and you don't need to come back again. Fair enough?"

Atwater thought he'd heard of worse deals, and he nodded. "When can I start?"

Henessey reached under the counter and tossed him an apron. "You just did," he said.

CHAPTER 9

Morgan put in a quiet few days at the store. The work wasn't hard, but he had never been easy around people. To break him in slowly, Henessey had him take inventory. "Get familiar with what we got," he told him. "Better to say we ain't got something than to have somebody wait around, then have to tell him you was wrong. People don't like that. They think you made fools of 'em."

"This is the only general store in town, Mr. Henessey," Morgan told him.

"I know it. And that's the way I want it. Keep 'em satisfied, they won't need another one. You go on now, count up everything and write it down. Then we can look it over together and see what we got to order."

So he did. He spent hours poking into the

corners of every shelf in the place, including the storage room in back. He saw more spiders than he knew existed in Wyoming territory, found three different nests full of baby mice, and one dead squirrel, probably brought in and hidden by Henessey's moth-eaten cat. The same cat that was supposed to be catching the mice. He also found a bat hanging upside down in the storeroom, up in a corner behind some bolts of dusty cloth.

But he didn't catch a single glimpse of Brett Kinkaid.

When he was out front, he'd try to get near the window every few minutes, to see if maybe Kinkaid was watching the place. On the morning of his fifth full day, he took a scrub pail and a sponge full of lye soap and vinegar and cleaned the front window inside and out. When he was finished, the window sparkled in the sun and he could see better than ever. But there was still no sign of Kinkaid.

It was Friday, he noticed a trickle of cowhands riding in, ones mostly, sometimes twos. They'd tie off in front of one of the half-dozen saloons, shamble inside, their bowed legs slowly adjusting to walking again, hitching up their pants and, one or two of them, adjusting their gunbelts.

He knew what was going through their heads. They were looking forward to something wet and something soft, in that order. And they weren't too particular about either. Four weeks' worth of dust took a lot of washing down, and turpentine would have done if there was nothing else available.

In the back of his mind was the thought, more like a hope, really, that Tom would come in for supplies. He wanted another chance to talk to the boy. Maybe if he saw his father in an apron he wouldn't be so standoffish, so resentful. Hell, looking at himself reflected in the clean glass of the window, he looked absolutely ordinary, just a man with an honest job, a little dirt on his hands, a little dust in his mustache. Certainly no one to be mad at or scared of.

That's what he thought.

Whether Tom would agree was something he'd have to wait to find out.

When Morgan came back inside after finishing the window, Lyle Henessey was taking off his apron. He smiled and asked, "Think you can handle the place alone for an hour?"

"I guess so," Morgan said, none too sure and hoping it didn't show.

Henessey shrugged into a suit coat and smoothed the lapels with his thick-knuckled hands. "We got a meeting. The merchant's association. Figger I ought to be there since I'm the vice president."

"Something going on?"

"What could be going on, Morgan?"

"I don't know. Just seemed like the middle of the day, a work day especially, is an odd time for a meeting."

"These boys are skittish, Morgan. They get fussy, like old maids, is all. See, most of 'em ain't done anything but wear aprons all their lives. Me, I done time in the war, and before I got here, I was a prospector for four years. Was in the Black Hills when Custer came through. That was a sight. That man knew what was what, Morgan."

"Didn't help him none at Little Big Horn."

"Wasn't his fault. But I don't have time to argue about it, now. Maybe tonight, after we close up shop. I'll buy you a beer and tell you what's what on that score. You get something you can't handle and what can't wait, we'll be in the back of the Methodist church, the east end of town. But I don't think that'll happen. In the meantime, you want, you can repaint that sign over the front. I got the paint three months ago. Never got around to it."

"Not much with a paintbrush, Mr. Henessey."

"Me neither, Morgan. But as long as folks can tell the name of the place, it'll be alright. Just follow what's already there. Only make it a little neater, if you can." Henessey laughed and pulled a fat cigar from his jacket pocket. He bit the end off it, lit it with a wooden match, and filled the store with a thick cloud of acrid smoke. "Leona don't let me smoke at home, and they stink up the store," he said, gesturing with the cigar. "Got to grab a smoke when I can. Be back in about a hour."

Henessey left trailing a wreath of the thick gray smoke. Morgan watched him until he was out of sight, then went in the back to find the paint.

He grabbed a ladder, tucked a brush into his back pocket, and hooked the paint pail by its handle. As he started toward the front, he heard the bell announce a customer, and struggled through the door, turning sideways to squeeze through with the ladder.

It was Brett Kinkaid.

"Marshal," Atwater said, setting the ladder down and bending to set the paint on the floor. He slipped behind the counter, wiping imaginary dust on his apron. "What can I do for you?"

Kinkaid reached into his pocket and took out a piece of paper. He smoothed it against his chest. It was a piece of newspaper that had been folded several times. Morgan could see the other side. It was some sort of advertisement for farm implements. When Kinkaid was satisfied with the smoothness, he set it down on the counter.

Morgan waited while Kinkaid sucked his lower lip, then stabbed the center of the creased paper with a finger. "A good likeness," he said. "You've held up pretty well."

"What are you talking about?"

"Look at it." He pivoted his finger on its tip, and the paper rotated a hundred and eighty degrees. "Go on, pick it up and look at it."

Morgan took the paper. On the front side was a grainy photograph of a younger Morgan Atwater. He knew the picture. Matthew Brady had taken it sixteen years before, in Texas. The great Civil War photographer had happened through Quiet Springs when he had been sheriff. The visit coincided with an attempted bank robbery in the aftermath of which Morgan had shot and killed three of the four would-be robbers.

The presence of Brady, who memorialized the events on a dozen plates, had turned an ordinary occurrence into one of those artificial moments of history. It was the beginning of Atwater's notoriety, and the end of his normal life. Sixteen years was a long time. But the past just wouldn't go away.

Kinkaid was watching him closely. "That *is* you, ain't it?"

"What if I say it is?"

"Whether you do or don't say don't make any difference. It's you, and we both know it. I knew you looked familiar. I just couldn't place it. So I passed the word. A friend down in Denver dug this up and sent it to me."

That explained why Kinkaid hadn't been around, Morgan thought. He had been waiting for the picture to arrive. He looked at Kinkaid, trying to read the man's mind. But he hadn't a clue. He said, "What about it?"

"Oh, come on, Atwater. It ain't every day a man gets to look a legend in the eye. And you're that, alright, a bonafide legend of the frontier. Least, that's what the story that comes with this here picture says. Now, ain't that something?"

"I wouldn't know."

"I'll bet you wouldn't."

"Marshal, I have some work to do, so if you don't mind..."

"Work, is it? What kind of work is this for a bonafidee legend? Storekeeper." Kinkaid shook his head as if he couldn't imagine a more precipitous descent from the heights of glory. "Well, since that's the line of work you're in now, you mind sellin' me something?"

"If we have it, of course."

"Oh, you have it, alright."

"What is it?"

"A box of Remington Arms .45 caliber cartridges. I know you got 'em, 'cause I buy 'em here all the time. One dollar and fifteen cents. Know it by heart." He tossed a handful of coins on the table and laughed when two skidded off the edge and clunked down behind it. "It's Friday, you know? Gonna need them shells. I can just tell. Always use a lot of ammunition on the weekend. But then, you already know about that, don't you? Bet you used to go through a box or two ever' weekend. Before you was a storekeeper, I mean."

Morgan ignored the baiting, turned to the shelves behind him, and found the ammunition. He hefted the dead weight in his hand, so much heavier than one would expect a small pasteboard box to be, then took a deep breath.

He turned back and set it on the counter with a heavy thump. "Anything else?"

"Seems like you pretty anxious to get rid of me, Morgan. You mind if I call you Morgan. I mean, I never been on a first name basis with a legend before. It'd make my mama proud."

"I'll bet she's already proud, Mr. Kinkaid."

The marshal didn't much like the tone, but he didn't know how to object, so he let it slide. "You do much shooting anymore, Morgan? You still lightning quick? Says in the paper you could hit a silver dollar at thirty yards. That right? Can you still do that?"

Morgan didn't say anything. Kinkaid tapped the box of bullets. "Be back next Monday for another box. You ain't got 'em in stock, you tell Lyle I said to get some more in."

"I'll do that, Marshal."

Kinkaid started for the door, then stopped. He

turned back a half step. "Listen, maybe you and me could have a contest. See who's the better shot. What do you say? Could be fun."

"I don't think so."

"Oh, I do. I surely do." He flipped a casual salute, touching the brim of his hat with extended fingers, and left.

Morgan ran a hand over his chin. He knew it might come to this, but not so soon. He cursed the past that followed him like a foal followed a mare. Then, knowing there wasn't anything much he could do that he hadn't already done, he looked back at the shelf. Six boxes of .45 shells were still there.

Morgan walked to the window after Kinkaid left. He tried to stay out of sight. Part of him wanted to rip through the door and call Kinkaid out right then, but he knew it was the wrong thing to do. If he was going to change his life, he would have to learn to control himself. Kinkaids were two bits a gross, and he couldn't kill them all. No matter how much he wanted to.

Then, as if he'd known all along that Morgan was watching him, the marshal turned and flipped another salute toward the store window. Even in the bright sunlight washing out his features, the broad grin was unmistakable. Morgan clenched his fist and slammed it into the window frame. He didn't even feel it.

He fished in his pocket, put a dollar fifteen in the till, and grabbed a box. He had a feeling he was going to need them.

CHAPTER 10

With the box of bullets in his hand, Morgan walked back to the window. Kinkaid was no longer in sight, but Morgan stared after the marshal for a long time. Finally, realizing he wasn't going to see him again, he moved to the back of the store.

He leaned back against the shelves behind the counter, wondering whether Kinkaid had just threatened him, or not. The mind-set of a man who lived with a gun in his hand was a peculiar one. Used to offense, he had a tendency to find one where none was intended. But Kinkaid was not a subtle man. And there had been nothing subtle about the exchange. Or had there been?

To get his mind off it, Morgan grabbed the ladder and the paint can. He walked out into the heat and unfolded the heavy wooden ladder. It was old, covered with drips of a dozen colors of paint, scarred and nicked on every rung. "It's seen almost as much wear and tear as I have," Morgan mumbled, as he knelt to open the paint. He took the can in both hands and shook it rapidly, like an angry parent trying to shake some sense into a wayward child.

When he was satisfied the paint would be mixed, he fished a pocket knife out of his jeans and pried the lid off. The paint was bright red. There were still a few swirls of oil on the surface, and he took the long-handled brush and stirred the top inch or two with the handle, wiped it off on a rag, and started up the ladder.

As he climbed, he found himself out in the bright sunlight. It felt warm on his back and the back of his neck. The sign was desperately in need of repainting, and Morgan scraped the last few flakes of the old blue lettering away with one callused palm.

Concentrating on the delicate demands of the job, he realized he'd be better off to take the sign down. He could control the brush better, and the paint wouldn't run. Shaking his head in annoyance, he climbed back down, set the paint on the board-walk alongside the door, and stepped back into the welcome shade of the store. It felt ten degrees cooler, at least, and he wiped beads of sweat off his forehead with one rolled-up shirtsleeve.

Henessey kept tools in the back. Morgan had seen them during his inventory. He found a hammer and a pair of pliers. They should do the trick. He was back outside and halfway up the ladder when the next cowhand rode past. Morgan watched him tie up and head into the Whistle Wetter Tavern.

The sign was down in fifteen minutes. He used an old canvas for a drop cloth, and got down on his hands and knees with a pencil to block out the letters. He was almost done when he saw Henessey up the street. The shop owner was talking to three men he didn't recognize. A little beyond the men, he saw a bright white steeple and realized the meeting must have just finished, spilling the men out into the street where a few of them continued talking.

As Morgan watched, Henessey lit another cigar and wreathed the four men in thick smoke. Morgan went back to his work and etched the last three letters in place. As he backed up to eyeball his handiwork, Henessey approached.

"Well, well, well. Knocked the darn thing right off the roof, did you, Morgan?" He laughed. "I didn't expect you to put so much work into that old sign. But now that I get a good look at it, I guess you got the right idea."

"I hope you don't mind, Mr. Henessey. But it was in pretty bad shape."

"Mind, course I don't mind. Lot of gumption you got, Morgan. You just might have been tailor made for the mercantile profession."

"I doubt that."

"Don't be so sure. Listen, I got some white paint in the back room. You might as well do the whole shebang, since you got off to such a good start. I can cover the store for the rest of the afternoon. If you don't mind, that is. I can even pay you a little on the side. Seems to me you didn't hire on as a

handy man and sign painter, too. Not for the wages
I offered."

"No need. I just thought I might as well do it
right if I was gonna do it at all."

"You thought right. Let me get you that paint."
He stepped up on the boardwalk, looked down at
the sign for a moment. "You got a right sharp eye.
Those letters are neat as a pin. You must have a
steady hand, Morgan."

Morgan smiled to himself. "You don't know
the half of it."

"What line of work were you in before you
come to Cross Creek?"

"Oh, this and that."

Henessey smiled. "You don't want to say, that's
fine by me. I always judge a man by what he does
next, not by what he done last. Seems to work out,
too."

Morgan nodded. He wasn't about to let himself
get drawn into some confessional autobiography.
He knelt by the signboard and darkened a couple
of the pencil lines as Henessey disappeared inside.
The shopkeeper was back in two minutes, his apron
on but untied, and a can of white paint in hand.

"This ought to spruce her up just fine," he said,
handing the paint down to Morgan. "I'll be inside,
you need me. Got some old calico you can use for
rags, if you need 'em."

"I'm all set, Mr. Henessey."

Henessey stopped in the doorway and looked
back over his shoulder. "Listen here, Morgan.
You're gonna work for me, you might as well call
me Lyle, like ever'body else."

"Yes, sir."

"And don't sir me. Just because I own this place, that don't mean I expect a grown man to bow down like some wet-behind-the-ears schoolboy."

"Whatever you say, Lyle."

"That's more like it, Morgan. When you done there, let me know. I'll give you a hand puttin' 'er back up, once the paint dries. Shouldn't take long in this dang heat." He mopped his brow and neck with a colorful handkerchief, then vanished again.

As Morgan worked, he could hear Lyle inside, humming in a big, off-key baritone. Every so often, another hand or two would drift in, find his favorite watering hole, and start on a long weekend. Some of the saloons were already getting loud as Morgan finished the white background. Lyle had been right, too, about the drying time. One end was already dry by the time he got to the other. He figured he'd take a fifteen-minute break and get some cold tea. By then, he should be able to do the lettering without worrying about the red paint running into the white.

The meticulous work was making him edgy. Everytime he finished a letter, he'd back away from the board. His hands would be stiff with tension, and the muscles in the back of his neck and in his jaw would be hard as buckshot.

It was near six o'clock when Henessey appeared in the doorway for the eighth time. "Are you still not done, Morgan? Jaysus, you're takin' the devil's own sweet time with that sign. Is it Leonardo I should be calling you, now? Will you be after jabberin' to me in Eyetalian now?"

"One more, Lyle. Just one more. It would have helped matters if your name was Ryan or Kelly."

Henessey laughed. "Well, if I stay here any longer, my name might not be any shorter, but the Missus will shorten something else of mine, something I treasure more than me name, if you know what I mean. Have you ever been married, Morgan?"

Atwater hesitated. Henessey noticed, but didn't press the issue. "I don't blame you. Many's the time I thought about skippin' out meself. I may one day yet."

Atwater turned away.

"Oh, now, Morgan. Don't be takin' on like that. You show me the married man doesn't make a joke like that now and then, and I'll show you a widower." He laughed again, then, some secret sensitivity in him struggling to the surface at long last, he closed his mouth and the door to the shop. But he was back a moment later, his jacket draped over his arm. It was still warm, and he was a big man, feeling a little the worse after a long day in the uncommon heat.

"I left you a key," he said, "with your first week's pay. It's by the cash drawer."

That was all, no ceremony, just a simple gesture, but it spoke volumes both about Henessey and about what he thought of his new employee. "I'll see you in the morning. Maybe you'll have the sign done by then, eh?" He was still laughing when he ducked around the corner and moved down the alley to pick up his horse tethered behind the shop.

There was a sudden horrendous roar, and Morgan turned to look up the street. The last bits of glass were cascading through the frame of The Hangin' Tree's front window. A cowboy lay on his back in the glittering shards, along with a broken chair. An instant later, another cowhand came through the window, this one feetfirst. He stood over the first, another chair raised over his head.

Someone shouted, and the cowboy turned to look back into the broken window. Morgan started to move, and out of the corner of his eye, he saw someone else moving from across the street. Unconsciously, he felt for his hip, then realized his gunbelt was coiled on a chair in the back of Henessey's shop. He stopped, confused by the unfamiliar emptiness along his thigh.

The figure to his right had crystallized into the figure of Brett Kinkaid. Despite the heat, the marshal was still wearing a jacket.

"Don't mix in this, Atwater," he said. "This is my problem. You tend to the store, like a good fellow."

Then Kinkaid stepped up the leading edge of the boardwalk in front of The Hangin' Tree. "Cowboy," he said, "you let go of that chair right now. Real easy. If it floats, you walk away. But if it don't, you got a night in the best jail in the county, courtesy of Cross Creek."

The cowboy shook his head. "This ain't none of your concern. I can handle this just fine."

"Put the goddamned chair down. Now!"

The cowboy tossed the chair back through the window. It skidded until it slammed into a table. Morgan heard the sound of breaking glass again, this time faint and insubstantial.

"Give me your gun, cowboy," Kinkaid snapped.

"No, sir, I won't. No cause."

"I got all the cause I need."

The cowboy made an exasperated whooshing sound, and shook his head from side to side. Things were out of control now, and he just didn't understand how it happened. Something flew through the shattered frame and landed on the glass shards. The noise startled him and he jerked suddenly.

Just that quickly, Kinkaid had fired twice. As if in slow motion, Atwater saw the young cowhand tumble back through the window and disappear. His face was a mask of profound incomprehension as his hands twitched in front of his suddenly bloody chest. It looked as if he were trying to understand how the bullets could have gotten past before he managed to pluck them out of the air.

"You bastard," Atwater shouted. He threw himself on Kinkaid and dragged him down. "What in the hell is wrong with you?"

Men spilled out of the saloon now, and pulled Atwater off the marshal. Kinkaid, his lip bloody where he had driven his teeth through the flesh, lay there panting. He licked his lips once, then again.

Atwater turned away, staring at the now-empty window frame as if he weren't quite sure he'd seen anything happen. Then he turned back to Kinkaid. "You didn't have to do that," he said. "What in the hell did you do that for."

"You saw it. He was going for his gun."

"The hell he was. Something spooked him and he reacted, that's all. You killed him for nothing, you stupid sonofabitch."

"Atwater, you mind your own damn business. Or I'll mind it for you."

"What are you going to do? You going to shoot me, too? Is that it? Well I don't have a gun and you don't have an excuse."

Kinkaid laughed. He licked his lip again, then said, "I will have."

CHAPTER 11

They were all there. Tate Crimmins, as usual, had been the first one to arrive. Tate was proud of being a man in a hurry. That was no surprise because Tate had yet to find anything about himself he couldn't be proud of. And without working too hard at it, either. He was the mayor, but it was really his money that had got him elected, that and his willingness to shout longer and louder than anybody else.

He was up front of the meeting hall, sitting at a table like a tweed Buddha as the rest of them filed in in ones and twos. He kept fussing with his mustache, twirling the ends of the bushy thing. He didn't wax it, and the first time people met him, they wondered whether they should ask where he got the wooly caterpillar perched under his nose. As soon as they got to know him, though, they were glad they had bitten their tongues. Tate had no sense of humor. He never told a joke and never laughed at one. Two hundred pounds of ill humor on a five-and-a-half-foot frame summed him up.

Schuyler Weems, the Methodist minister, was there, too. It was his church they were using, and they were using it mostly because Tate had built the damn thing in the first place, then bought Weems to run it. Weems was a rail of a man, his spindly arms and legs like sticks inside his black suit. With his pasty skin and sunburned neck, he looked like he earned a little extra by hanging on a couple of sticks in somebody's cornfield when church wasn't in session.

Two of the others, Pete Jarnigan and Milosz Wickowski, were there because their businesses were starting to suffer. Lyle Henessey was there, too, mostly out of curiosity. He already knew what the problem was. He had warned Tate it was going to happen long before it had. And Warren Brewster, a little round man in a white shirt and sleeve garters, a smear of ink on his forehead, stood in the rear of the hall. He wasn't a member of the merchant's association, but he knew them all, and disliked most of them. Running the paper for six years, he had learned to ignore the things he didn't like as long as they didn't affect the public welfare. But this was something he couldn't overlook. While he watched and waited, he kept tugging on the prematurely gray sideburns that he had been cultivating since Yale.

Tate was getting restless. He was, as usual, in a hurry, and as mayor, he took things like agendas and schedules more seriously than most. He reached forward for the hand-carved gavel, rapped it on the hard wooden sole plate, and let it down with a clatter. He cleared his throat, and Warren Brewster reached for his pencil.

"Alright, let's get this over with. You people are wasting time."

"The hell we are. It's easy for you to say," Wickowski sputtered. "It don't hurt your business. Me, it hurts mine, my business."

The others shook their heads in agreement. Tate, who owned the bank, was only too aware that most of the rest of the members owed him money to one degree or another. Wickowski had touched a nerve. "Come on, Miles, it ain't that bad."

"Damn it, Tate. How many times I tell you. Pronounce it Milosh. That's my name."

"Whatever."

"My front window is gone."

"And the man who done it is in a pine box. It won't happen again."

"You tell us Kinkaid would make sure it doesn't happen again. But it happens again and again. He don't stop things. He shoots people after they break something."

Henessey said, "Maybe Tate's got a secret plan. Maybe he figgers Kinkaid'll kill all the trouble makers. *Then* we have law and order. That it, Tate?"

"Lyle, dammit, you know that ain't it. I want Cross Creek to be as quiet as any of the rest of you do. But it takes a while. You know that. You all knew that when we hired Kinkaid. He's doin' alright, you ask me."

"You ask *me*, I'd say the only one who's doing

alright is Wade Murtagh." Henessey nodded his head toward the town's funeral director. Murtagh beamed. It was like getting free advertising.

"You're all overreacting, Lyle. Kinkaid's doing what we hired him to do. He's doing his job. That's all there is to it."

"Six men in two months, Tate. Six! Now who's really overreacting here?"

"What do you want me to do. Turn the town back over to the thugs? You think that would help your businesses. Let's face it, Cross Creek has got to be civilized sooner or later. When it is, your businesses will adjust to it, they'll survive, they'll even flourish. All I'm trying to do is have that happen sooner, rather than later."

"And if I lose my customers, who forecloses on the mortgage, Tate?" Jarnigan barked. "Or do you send Kinkaid around to evict me with his gun, and drum up a little more business for Wade, while he's at it?"

"That's ridiculous, Pete. Don't make a fool of yourself, now."

"I'll tell you what I want you to do, Tate," Henessey said.

Crimmins groaned audibly. "What's that, Lyle?"

"I want you to fire his ass. Get him the hell out of town. The man's a menace. He's out of control."

"No, I won't do it."

"Won't, or can't? You afraid of him, too, Tate? Is that what this is all about? You a hostage along with the rest of us?"

"Don't be so melodramatic, Lyle. Nobody's hostage here. Nobody! Those six men he killed, they all made the first move. They all went for their guns before he ever drew. You know that as well as I do. Hell, most of you have been there at least once."

Warren Brewster interrupted from the back. "Why don't you get the Reverend Weems to tell us what he thinks? Forget about the business side. What's the Christian thing to do here, Reverend?"

"Shut up, Warren. You ain't a member," Crimmins bellowed. "You got no right to speak here."

Jarnigan stamped his foot on the ground and got up out of his chair. "Brewster's right. I want to hear what Reverend Weems has to say."

The minister, looking more like a scarecrow than ever, stood up. His hands shook as he brushed at wisps of hair behind his ears. "I agree with Mr. Crimmins," he said. He swallowed hard, then sat down as if his legs had suddenly evaporated.

Henessey waved a hand in disgust. "Exemplary Christianity, Reverend. And, I must say, courage unlike any the world has seen since Alexander breathed his last."

"You needn't get personal, Mr. Henessey."

"Shut up, Schuyler," Crimmins barked. "Now, unless there is any further discussion necessary, I think…"

"There is Tate, there surely is."

"What is it, Lyle?"

"I think we ought to vote on it. See whether enough of us want to see the ass end of this bastard's horse."

The door opened behind him, and Henessey turned to see what was going on. The newcomer stood in the door, his features obliterated by the wash of bright sun spilling in around him.

"You gonna vote on something that concerns me, seems like the decent thing to do would be to invite me, don't you think?" Kinkaid's voice was razor sharp. It echoed from the corners of the high-ceilinged room.

"This doesn't concern you, Kinkaid," Henessey said.

"The hell it doesn't."

"You don't belong here."

"Hey, Lyle, it's a free country. I want to watch the local muckedymucks at work, I got a right. Democracy in action." He stepped inside, spurs jingling, and moved past Henessey, then turned and faced him. "The way I see it, you men were about to vote on whether or not I still have a job here. Fact is, you ought to know I got a contract. All legal and proper, signed by your mayor, assures me one year of employment as town marshal. Now, anybody . . ."

"Contract?" Henessey spluttered. "Tate, is that right? You gave him a contract?"

"He wanted guarantees, we wanted him. That's what it took, so that's what I did."

"How come you didn't tell any of us about it?"

"No need. You told me what you all wanted. As mayor, I had the authority, and I did what had to be done. I daresay, none of the rest of you would have acted so decisively."

"You stupid, insufferably arrogant bastard! Don't you even see what you've done?" Henessey roared. "You've given the man a license to kill other men, and you can't revoke the damned license. Crimmins, you're a fool."

"Remember who you're talking to, Henessey..."

"Oh, don't you worry. I'll not forget that, not for a long, long time. This is one for the family saga, this is."

"Gents, I'll leave you to your business," Kinkaid said. He tipped his hat and walked slowly toward the front door again. He stopped with one hand on the door frame and turned. "Of course, you could always offer to buy my contract. I might be willing to waive my rights. But I don't come cheap, as you know. Good morning."

He was gone, but the foul taste he left in their mouths, all but Crimmins', lingered. Tate still didn't see what all the uproar was about. His cheeks were still red, annoyed as he was at Henessey's insults. But as far as he was concerned, everything was in order.

Kinkaid's announcement had taken more than a little wind out of the merchant's association's already tattered sails. Henessey pushed for a vote, and he got it. But no one wanted to tell Kinkaid he was fired, and if one of them did, no one wanted to pay him what it would cost.

They were stuck. Henessey delivered a tirade, trying to force the issue, but in the end, they just shook their heads. He warned them there would be more shooting, that maybe Kinkaid wouldn't stop at rowdy cowboys, that maybe one of their own family members might run afoul of the increasingly irascible marshal.

But nobody gave a damn except Lyle Henessey.

He left the meeting already hot under the collar. When he saw the marshal waiting across the street, it did nothing to cool him off. Henessey didn't respond to Kinkaid's pleasant wave, but the marshal fell in beside him anyway.

"So, Mr. Henessey, you don't much like me, do you?"

"It's not a question of what I like, Mr. Kinkaid. It's a question of what's right. And this town is a long way from right, at the moment. You were supposed to protect it, not destroy it."

"Sometimes you have to destroy something in order to save it, Lyle. Maybe you can't understand that, but I can. You can take your choice. You can have me, or you can have the barbarians. But you can't have both."

"I prefer the barbarians, thank you, Mr. Kinkaid."

"Course," the marshal said, stopping so abruptly that Henessey, in spite of his desire to leave the marshal behind, stopped in his tracks and looked back at Kinkaid, "there is another way."

"Oh, and what might that be?"

"Talk to Mr. Atwater. He'll know."

CHAPTER 12

Saturday nights were always the worst. No longer interested and, for all he knew, no longer even able to belt down a fifth of whiskey, cheap or otherwise, Morgan still sometimes got the urge. The lower he was, the higher he wanted to get. It had been a long time since he'd given in, and he wasn't about to do it now, not when he'd come so far and achieved so very little of what he'd come to do.

So he sat in his hotel room. The window was open, and he could hear the raucous clash of pianos, the shouts of drunken cowhands, and the restless galloping of horses whose riders were an inch from senseless with their untrammeled celebration. He thought a beer might be nice, but there was no way in hell he was prepared to risk a confrontation with Brett Kinkaid.

A prisoner, that's what he was. He stared at himself in the mirror, and was so depressed by what he saw he lay back on the bed and closed his eyes. He tried to drown out the sound of Saturday night in full swing. When that didn't work, he tried to drown himself in it, letting the boisterous clamor wash over him in wave after wave, hoping that, sooner or later, he would no longer even hear it.

There had to be some way to deal with Kinkaid that wouldn't require him to pick up a gun. For the last three days, he hadn't even worn it to Henessey's store. If Kinkaid wanted to shoot him in the back, there was nothing he could do about it anyway, and if the marshal was simply going to push and push and push until Morgan had no patience left, then it was best he didn't have a gun. He could take Kinkaid apart with his bare hands. And unless things changed for the better and soon, he had no doubt he would do just that.

Lying there as the sun set, spilling its bloody light through the delicate lace curtains, printing a pattern like ruby snowflakes on the bedspread, and on his bare chest and the backs of his hands, he retraced his footsteps for yet one more try at reconstructing a past that had somehow come to dominate his future.

There had to be a way to get Katie to listen to him. He realized he hadn't even told her about the money. But he had held back, not wanting her to think he was trying to pay for his mistake with cash, or to buy her back. And he knew her well enough to know that that's exactly what she would think.

And as for Tom, well, that was probably his biggest mistake. When the boy showed up, he had been caught off balance and never did get his feet back on the ground.

Thinking about his family was like trying to imagine the lives of two strangers. What were they doing at that moment, he wondered. And he admitted to himself that he didn't even know enough about them to make a credible guess. It would be easier to envision dinner at Tate Crimmins's house, or Lyle Henessey's, than to picture what his wife and son were doing while he lay there like a relic, one that didn't realize it was already dead, just unburied.

Morgan sat up and reached for a shirt hanging on the back of a chair. He had to get out of the room. The air was too thick, suffocating him with its stagnant heat. He should be alright, as long as he left his gun in his room. He ran a fistful of fingers across his chin, felt the stubble, and decided to let it be. He didn't trust himself with a razor at the moment.

He buttoned the shirt, tucked it in, and got to his feet. He was heading for the door when he heard a knock. He stopped in his tracks, his eyes instantly searching out the Colt .45, nestled like a rattler in its leather coils. He started toward it, changed his mind, and headed back for the door as someone knocked a second time.

"Who is it?" As if Kinkaid would announce himself like an expected guest.

Again a knock, and again he called, "Who is it?"

"It's me. Tom."

He reached for the door with one trembling hand, bracing himself on the door frame with the other arm. As the door swung back, he stepped away, still not sure he'd heard rightly.

But he had. "Can I come in?" Tom asked.

"Hell yes, sure, of course. Come in, son."

Tom flinched at the last word, his eyes flickering as if he'd been sucker punched by a master. He hesitated, then crossed cautiously over the threshold, like a man knowing he's taking an irretrievable step.

"Sit down," Morgan said, indicating the lone chair in the sparsely furnished room. "I'm glad you've come."

"I'm not so sure I should have."

"Why not?"

"You know the answer to that."

"Look, Tommy, I . . ."

"It's Tom."

"Alright then, Tom. If you came here to accuse me of being a bad father, you're wasting your time. It's true. I admit it. I know it better than you, and I have to live with that knowledge in a way you can't imagine."

"I have enough pain of my own. I'm not here because I want to be."

"Why then?"

"Because my mother asked me to come. That's the only reason."

"So . . ." Morgan let out a long, slow breath. His next words were going to be critical. They might even govern the rest of his life in a way he could

not foresee. He reached into his pocket for his tobacco pouch, and nodded to his son for a moment
of indulgence while he rolled a cigarette. When it
was finished, he couldn't seal the cylinder because
his mouth was too dry. Walking to the night table,
he took a glass, filled it with water from a pitcher,
and took a sip. He licked the paper, squeezed the
cigarette tightly enough to wasp it in the middle,
and stuck it in his mouth.

The match filled the room with its sharp scent,
and Tom watched his father's shaking hand move
the still sputtering matchhead toward the cigarette.
With his lungs full of smoke, Morgan said, "I'm a
little nervous."

"I thought you didn't *get* nervous. I thought
that was your claim to fame."

"I have no fame, Tom, claimed or otherwise.
I never wanted to be well known. I hated the notoriety, every damned minute of it."

"Then why did you do what you did?"

"That's a long story."

"I have time."

"Yes, you do. I don't know if I do, though.
Not enough, anyway." He felt it slipping away again.
In his mind, he could replay his life. Every mistake,
every error in judgment, every misstep, came back
to him in one continuous stream of well-meaning
ineptitude. How do you explain that to an eighteen-
year-old boy, he wondered. How can you make
him understand how much it hurts to know how
badly you played the one hand you had been dealt?

"If you'd rather I come back another time..."

"No, don't leave. I just..." He shook his head.

"Look, I don't know how much you know about me. Maybe I should start there."

"Start wherever you want. You don't have to explain yourself to me, because I don't really give a good god damn. You know?"

Morgan tilted his head back slowly until he was staring at the ceiling. He felt his eyes mist over, and he swallowed hard, trying to clear the blur before looking at his son again. "You drink?"

"Beer. Sometimes."

"Can I buy you a beer?"

As anxious as his father to get out of the room, which seemed to be shrinking by the second, Tom nodded. "Why not?"

As Morgan stood up, he glanced again at the gunbelt on the table. Tom saw the glance, looked at the gunbelt, then at Morgan. His face had gone cold. When Morgan moved for the door, Tom said, "Aren't you forgetting something?"

"No."

Tom looked at the gunbelt again, but didn't say anything.

Morgan opened the door. He held it for Tom, turned the lamp down, and let the door close behind him. In the hallway, Morgan walked behind his son. The boy was big and going to be bigger. He was already an inch taller than Morgan, and probably had a little growing to do. He would fill out some, his shoulders broaden a bit, his arms thicken a little.

They walked down the wide stairs side by side. In the lobby, Morgan glanced back up the stairs as if debating going back up. "Change your mind?" Tom asked.

Morgan opened the front door and stepped out into the street. The sun was gone now, and there was a breeze, little more than a hot breath, but at least the air was moving. "You have a favorite place, Tom?"

"Nope. This is your field, not mine."

Morgan crossed the street and headed for Largo's, the same bar he'd been in before. It was crowded but not, he knew, as crowded as The Hangin' Tree would be. Inside, they found a couple of empty tables, and Morgan led the way to one in a corner, as far away from the piano as they could get. Nobody looked up when they entered, and when they sat down, Morgan felt more comfortable, surrounded as they were by people who paid them no attention. It seemed somehow better than being face-to-face alone. Looking around would not seem so blatant an evasion here.

A waiter in a striped shirt took their order. When he was gone, Tom tapped his fingertips on the table. "Why did you come back?" he asked.

"I . . . a lot of reasons, really. I wanted to see you. I wanted to see your mother again. I thought I owed it to you both."

"*Owed* it to us? What in hell did we do to deserve it?"

"Is that what you think? You think I want to punish you both somehow? Is that what my presence is? Is that all it means to you?"

The waiter reappeared, set the two mugs on the table, and took the silver dollar Morgan shoved across the damp wood. When he was gone, Tom said, "We had it all worked out, you know, Mom and me. We were in control of our lives. We knew who we were. We knew how our lives were going to be. You ruined all that. Just by showing up, you wrecked it all."

"That wasn't my intention."

"Maybe not, but my mother has cried herself to sleep every night for a week. She never did that before. Not ever."

Morgan thought about the emphasis. Tom was probing, looking for a chink in Morgan's armor. And he'd found it. Katie. Always Katie. "Maybe she should have. Maybe she can let herself get rid of a lot of bottled-up anger now, anger she should have gotten rid of a long time ago."

"No, that's where you're wrong. That kind of anger you don't ever want to get rid of. It keeps you safe."

"What about you? You're angry, I know that. But have you ever let yourself feel it, or do you always have to be in control? Safe . . . as you say."

"Is that what I am, in control? Funny, it sure as hell doesn't feel as good as it should."

Morgan sipped his beer slowly.

"Son, I . . ."

"Don't call me that." Tom shoved the beer across the table. The glass smacked into Morgan's, cracked, and spilled its contents all over the table. "Look, my mother wants you to come to dinner tomorrow. One o'clock."

"Your mother does. But not you."

"No. Not me."

"I see."

"The hell you do."

CHAPTER 13

Morgan didn't sleep all night. He spent hours looking out the hotel window, watching the night life, so very different from the daytime quiet. So different, too, from what the leading citizens of Cross Creek thought it should be. The difference was not just night and day. It was the difference between the serene barrenness of a flat rock and the teeming scurry when you pried it up and flipped it over. Just as pill bugs and spiders, ants and centipedes crawled and crept on secret business, so too did the cowhands and the women who preyed on them.

Morgan had done his share of pub crawling. And he had made a living for a while riding herd on the pub crawlers. He knew what was going on. But he knew it was more harmless than Tate Crimmins believed. He realized that what upset Crimmins was not what the cowhands and their floozies were doing, but that he didn't control it. The squeaky morality of men like Crimmins was usually less about the actuality of sin than it was about the appearance.

The irony, one that so far seemed to escape just about everyone but Lyle Henessey, was that Brett Kinkaid, hiding behind the shiny badge Tate Crimmins had pinned on him, didn't give a damn about either. He was obsessed with self-aggrandizement. Every tombstone he planted was another stepping stone up the side of Olympus. The way he saw it, you kill enough high-spirited, liquored-up cowboys, and you got to the top.

Morgan Atwater had climbed partway up the same mountain. He had gotten close enough to see there was nothing on top except a rocky path down the other side. The thing about a man like Kinkaid was you couldn't tell him anything. He knew what was what. He had to see for himself. And he had a kind of logic on his side. If you'd never been there, what did you know? And if you had, you were just jealous. Nice, neat, logical.

And dead wrong.

But Morgan was selfish, too. He hadn't come here to save Cross Creek from itself. He'd come here to salvage that little bit of himself that was worth saving and, in the process, just maybe rescue the one dream he'd never given up on.

By the time the sun came up, he was already dressed. Kate wanted him to come. He wrestled with that knowledge, tried to guess her motives, and could find none, at least none that he would allow himself to accept. But it didn't matter. She wanted him to come. It couldn't be bad.

If he could get her on his side, he might have a chance to win Tom's trust. He would settle for indifference at first. It had to be hard for the boy. But if he had a chance, that would be enough. He was determined to make it right.

He walked downstairs and out into the bright sunshine. Sitting on the porch of the hotel, he watched the families in their Sunday best making their way to the town's two churches. He wondered what it felt like, taking your son by the hand, your wife on your arm, everything stiff, the unyielding collar biting into your neck, your face red from the razor's scrape. Maybe even a squirt of witch hazel.

He remembered going to church with his father once. The old man's Sunday tweed whispering with every step, the smell of bay rum surrounding him like a cloud. And the bees, coming close, drawn by the fragrance, circling around the brim of his father's Sunday hat and buzzing angrily when they found no flower. He had been small then, looking up the legs of this stern and strange man whose massive hand swallowed his five-year-old fingers, the hand itself, and half the wrist.

He felt as if he were in the grip of some omnipotent being who had taken his father's place during the night, wore his clothes that bright Sunday morning. Whoever it was looked like his father, and sounded like him. If you didn't know any better, you'd have sworn it was James Atwater and little Morgan. Lily was there, too, a mound of red curls under a black hat. Both perched atop a larger mound of whispering linen, her feet impossibly tiny in black shoes with a dozen buttons up the front. And she kept looking at her son, her hot fingers fussing with the curls over Morgan's tight collar.

He remembered the long service, the minister high in a wooden pulpit thumping his fist, beating it like a drum. The resounding thumps echoed from the bare rafters for nearly an hour. It had seemed so strange to him. He knew the man in the black suit and the tight white collar, too. But like his mother and father, something had changed Frank Dillard. Instead of the rawboned farmer who cussed like a stevedore and snapped his galluses before cutting loose with a stream of tobacco juice, he was some kind of demon.

He had thundered about Satan and his minions, only too willing to skin them all alive and strip the flesh from their bones with beaks and scaly talons. There was no pain like that of fire, he shouted, warning them all of the fires of hell ready to spring through the floorboards and reduce them to cinders. And there was no escape for the evil man. The fire and the ravening beasts would get them all. He had scared Morgan so badly, Lily had to take him outside.

Afterward, his father ruffled his hair and told him not to worry, that Frank just got carried away when he preached. But they hadn't taken him back to church for years. His father even stopped going half the time, leaving Lily to save them all. And she had done her damnedest, Morgan thought.

Watching these people on their way to salvation, he wondered what went through their minds.

When the rush died to a trickle, Morgan went inside and took a table at the restaurant window. He ate slowly, thinking more than he should, and left half his food. The waitress seemed insulted, and he tried to explain that it was him, not the food, that there was nothing wrong with the meal. She didn't seem convinced.

Milton was at the stable door, another pile of chips in his lap. He looked at Atwater with a curious smile. "Ain't you going to church, Atwater?"

"Not much on churchgoing, Mr. Milton."

"Me neither. But then, I don't need savin' as much as some folks do."

Atwater laughed. "I reckon I'm long past saving, Mr. Milton."

"You want your horse?"

Atwater nodded. "You stay there. I'll get him." He went on inside and saddled the big bay. Tugging the reins, he walked the animal outside and swung into the saddle.

"Nice day for a ride, Atwater."

"I hope so."

"But you be careful." He got up, brushed the shavings from his wrinkled lap, and walked close to Atwater. With one hand on the reins, he said, "I don't like what's going on. But I can't do nothing about it. Crimmins and them has made a fair mess of things. You make sure you don't get ground up in it. Understand?"

"Thanks. But I don't think there's anything to worry about, Mr. Milton."

"You're a fool, then." He turned back to his chair, the knife blade catching the sunlight and flashing on the door. Without turning, he said, "I was you, I'd do myself and this town a favor and put one right through Brett Kinkaid's heart. He don't deserve no better, and he'll do it to you, he gets the chance."

He sat down again and started whittling.

The ride to Katie's gave him time to think, the last thing he needed. He'd already been doing too much thinking. He felt a funny prickle along his spine, and the hairs on the back of his neck were bristling. He didn't know whether it was because of Milton's warning, or something more immediate.

As he crested the last ridge overlooking Katie's spread, he turned in the saddle. Looking back and down through the tall grass and the swaths of bright flowers he saw a rider come over the last ridge. The distance was too great, even without the blinding sunlight, to tell who it was. He thought about Kinkaid, but had never seen the marshal on a horse, so the mount meant nothing to him.

The rider was taking his time, letting his horse walk at its own pace. Morgan was sure the man was following him, but it was a free country, and he was afraid of seeming paranoid. If it was Kinkaid, he would just let the man know his pressure was working. If it wasn't, he'd make a fool of himself. So he shrugged and rode on down the hill.

Tom was on the porch when he rode up. The boy nodded, but said nothing. Katie came out on the porch. She smoothed her dress down the front, then tucked a few strands of hair behind her right ear. It looked like she was wearing makeup, and he was tempted to comment. But when he opened his mouth, Tom looked at him sharply, and he settled for a wave.

Slipping from the saddle, he tied up at the corral fence, close enough to the trough for the bay to drink. As he walked back to the porch, Katie smiled. "You're early. Couldn't wait to see me, Morgan?"

Tom got up in disgust and stomped off the porch.

"Tom," she said, "you come right back here this minute."

"Let him go, Katie."

"I didn't raise him to have bad manners, Morgan."

"I didn't raise him at all, and that's what he's mad about. Besides, there's a difference between good manners and lying through your teeth. The boy doesn't want to pretend. I think he's right."

She started to object, then shook her head. "You're right," she said, "I just wanted things to . . ."

"Me, too," he said. "But we've got to learn all over again."

"Learn what?" She cocked her head, half grinning and half scowling.

"To be civil."

"Oh." She seemed disappointed.

"You look wonderful," he said.

"It's a new dress. I just finished it last night. I thought I might as well try it on."

"It suits you."

"Thank you, Morgan." She seemed flustered, then turned to open the screen door. "Come in," she said. "I have coffee up."

It was cooler inside, and Morgan looked for a place to hang his hat. Kate stepped close to him and took it. She circled the hat by its brim, watching her hands move. She looked up at him then. "I'm sorry about the other day," she said.

"I guess I surprised you some."

She smiled. "Some."

"You know, I don't want to upset you or Tom. It's just that..."

"I always believed you'd come back, you know. In the beginning, I knew it, really. But then, when you were gone so long...I didn't know what to believe. I started to think you were dead." She looked away again, and set his hat on the table. When she turned back, she threw herself at him, pounding him with both fists. "Damn you, Morgan, how could you do it? Why? Why?"

He wrapped his arms around her and held her until she calmed down. She looked up at him, her mouth slightly open, waiting. "It's a long story, Katie."

"Then you better start talking," she said. She extricated herself and backed toward a chair.

He stood there, trying to decide what to do with his hands. Finally, he stuck them in his back pockets. "I had a reputation," he began. "You knew that. But what you didn't know was that it was a millstone. I didn't want it and I didn't know how to get rid of it. So I tried to run away from it. Changed my name, changed the way I looked. But it didn't make any difference. Somebody always found me. Then, once I knew I couldn't run, I was ashamed to come back. And I was worried about you and

Tom. Someday, somebody was going to come along and kill me. I didn't want you to have to live with that certainty. So..."

There was a footstep on the porch. He flinched. "It's just Tom," Katie told him.

Then a knock, gently at first, then harder.

"He knock to come into his own house?" Morgan asked.

She shook her head. "I'll get it." She went to the door and opened it.

From where he stood, Morgan couldn't see the visitor.

"Anything the matter?" Katie asked.

"I don't know, ma'am. Thought I'd better stop and see, though. Mind if I come in?"

Katie backed away to make room. It was Brett Kinkaid. He smiled at Morgan. "So, Mr. Atwater, what brings you out this way? Sunday visit, is it?"

"None of your business, Kinkaid."

"Well, I don't know about that." He turned to Katie. "You know this is a very famous man, ma'am? Very famous. Yessir, and very dangerous, too. A gunfighter of more than passing repute. Not sure you ought to allow him in your home, 'specially without your husband here."

Kate looked puzzled. She looked at Morgan, who shook his head slightly. Turning back to Kinkaid, she said, "But my husband is here, Marshal."

"Oh, is that right, Mrs....?"

"Atwater," she said. "Mrs. Morgan Atwater."

"I see."

"Now, if there's nothing more you want, we were about to sit down for dinner."

"No, ma'am. Nothing more. For now. I guess I'll see you again, though."

Kinkaid smiled broadly, tipped his hat, and nodded to Morgan. "Mr. Atwater," he said.

When he was gone, Katie sat down slowly. "What was that all about?" she asked.

"That was my past, turning into my future."

CHAPTER 14

Katie was clearing away the dishes. Tom sat, still sulking, his elbows braced on the table and his chin cupped in his hands. The meal had been tense, even hostile at times, as Tom continually sniped at his father. Morgan had done his best to defuse the situation, but Tom was unrelenting.

In desperation, Morgan had brought up the letter of credit. He hadn't wanted to mention it until some of the smoke had cleared. He wanted Katie to get used to him, at least a little. He wanted Tom to accept if not forgive him. But it was beginning to look like there was no possibility of that happening.

"I don't need the money, Morgan," Kate was saying. "I do alright here."

"You can always use it. Maybe you can add to

the spread. Maybe you'll have a bad year. Maybe anything . . . you know?"

"What he means is he wants us to forgive him, and he thinks he knows our price," Tom said. He didn't even bother to lift his head, and the words came out garbled, as if he had a mouth full of caramel.

"It's not for you to decide, son," Morgan said.

"That's the story of my life, isn't it. I don't get to decide anything. I get to sit around and let people who don't give a damn about me make all my decisions."

"Thomas, maybe you should go to your room," Kate snapped.

"Really? You mean it's still mine? I thought maybe you were going to ask me to move out, so he could live here."

Kate swung wildly, but she still managed to clip him on the side of his head. "You shut up. Who in the hell do you think you are? This is still my house, and you are still my son. You do what I tell you."

Tom stood up. He didn't touch his face, but it must have hurt. The imprint of Katie's fingers was clearly visible in front of his right ear. There was a bright red outline surrounding a stark white impression.

"Maybe I better go," Morgan said.

"Why don't you," Tom mumbled.

"Morgan, stay. Maybe we should take the time to work this through. We'll never get to the end of it if you come and go."

"That's what he does best, Mother. Or have you forgotten already?"

Kate was on the edge of exploding. Morgan knew he couldn't afford to have mother and son at each other's throats. He put up a hand and said, "I think maybe it's been too long an afternoon for all of us. I should head back. I have to be at work early in the morning."

"Work? You mean you're planning on staying in Cross Creek? Why didn't you say something?"

"It never . . . I mean, it just didn't come up, I guess."

"Where are you working?"

"At Henessey's General Store."

"Lyle's a good man," Katie said.

"I've got no complaints."

"That makes one of us," Tom said. Without waiting for a rebuke from his mother, he stomped toward the door and was out of sight before it closed behind him.

"You have to forgive him," Katie said. "Morgan, I'm worried about him. He's so . . . volatile."

"Can't blame him, Katie."

"He's like you were when you were younger. Maybe still are, for all I know. So ready to take offense. And he doesn't forgive or forget easily."

"So I see."

"He'll come around. I just wish that . . ."

"What?"

"I wish he could have known you better. Before. You know? I mean, if he had some good memories, something to balance all the bitterness, maybe he'd . . ."

"Katie, he may never come around. God knows, he's got little reason to forgive me. No more than you . . ."

"But I have, Morgan. I . . . that man, the one who was here, the marshal . . ."

"What about him?"

"What did he mean when he said I'd be seeing him again?"

Morgan sighed. "I don't know, Katie. Just hot air, I think. Just talk."

"No, it wasn't just talk. It was much more than that. He was threatening you, wasn't he?"

Morgan stretched his neck to relieve some of the tension, but it was useless. He could feel the knots big as minié balls when he twisted his head.

"Tell me the truth, Morgan," Katie insisted.

"I don't know, Katie. I guess maybe he thinks . . . well, I don't know what he thinks. But he's trying to provoke me. I guess he wants me to come after him."

"But why?"

"Katie, don't you see? That's what my life has been like, long before I left you and Tom, that's what it was like. When I was sheriff down in Tulares, that man I . . . the one I . . . killed. He was just like Kinkaid. They get this funny idea that the bigger the target, the bigger they are if they can knock it down. That photographer, Brady, and the newspapers, once they started to write about me, that was the beginning."

"And it hasn't ended yet, has it?"

"I guess not. No."

"What are you going to do?"

"What can I do, Katie? I have two choices. I can let him run me off, or I can take him up on his offer. What I wanted was to find some middle ground. I thought if I could find a place where I wouldn't budge, but wouldn't be pushed, either, then maybe I could bury it all. But I can't . . . not yet, anyhow."

"I don't want you to leave, Morgan. We have too much to work out."

"I won't leave, Katie."

"Promise me . . ."

Morgan nodded. "I promise." He placed a finger to her lips, whether for a kiss or to silence her he wasn't sure. Maybe both, he thought. "Thanks for dinner. It was perfect. I'll find my own way out."

"Morgan, be careful."

Outside, he saw Tom on the far side of the fence. The boy must have heard the squeak of the door hinges. He turned and when he saw Morgan he started to run. Morgan watched until the boy was out of sight. He had a fleeting impulse to run after the boy, but realized that it couldn't work like that. Tom was going to have to come to him, whenever he was ready. If he ever was.

Back in the saddle, he felt as if everything was coming apart. Katie seemed conciliatory, even warm, but Tom was more distant. Without intending to, he was driving a wedge between them. And now Kinkaid knew he had a family. The realization froze his heart, the blood in his veins turned to ice, and his spine felt as if it had been plunged into snow melt.

He kicked the bay harder than he intended,

and the horse, in surprise, fairly leapt into a dead run. He took the road at a full gallop, not even slowing as he passed through the gate and headed into the long, winding path up the hillside. He glanced once over his shoulder at the house. It looked like Katie might be in the doorway, behind the screen, but he couldn't be sure.

He kept an eye out for his son, but saw only a meandering ditch of bent grass to mark where Tom had been. The twisted blades turned their undersides to the sun, filling the channel with a sheet of undulating silver. When he reached the ridge, he slowed to a walk and looked back down at the house. What at first viewing had seemed almost picturesque in its tranquility now seemed small and impossibly vulnerable.

He saw a figure struggle down the hill to the creek bed and across, then up the far bank. It was Tom. Even at long range, there was no mistaking him. He watched as Tom stomped through the grass on the far side, on up the steps, across the porch, and into the house. The boy never looked back.

He kicked the bay in the ribs again, again too hard. He pushed the mount at full tilt for nearly a mile. The hot wind slashed at his face and swept his breath away. His lips were twisted away from gritted teeth, and his jaw felt as if it would never unlock. Alternately he prodded the bay with his spurs and lashed it with the reins.

The pounding of the animal's hooves echoed inside his skull and he felt his heart slowly match the rhythm, attacking his chest like an incessant battery of siege guns. He wondered that his ribs didn't shatter and burst through his skin.

Morgan was still running flat out when he heard the first distant crack. It was almost swept away by the wind rushing past him. It sounded small, like a tiny pair of hands clapping once, then falling silent. He turned his head, unsure he had heard anything at all. Nudging the horse a little faster, he angled off the road and toward a stand of cottonwoods, their tall, slender trunks looking like bones from which the flesh had been dissolved.

He heard a second clap as he drew near the trees, then a third. Something slammed into one of the cottonwood trunks. He saw a small chip of bark cut loose, skid like a broken kite, flipping over once, then again, and finally disappearing and, as if it were the result of the bark hitting the ground, a fourth tiny clap.

Only then did he put it all together. Someone was shooting at him. A bullet had sliced the bark loose and the fourth clap had been the sound of the gunshot, lagging behind the slug. It was long-range shooting, judging by the gap between the bullet and the sound of the shot.

He jerked the reins and slipped out of the saddle while the horse skidded to a halt at the edge of the grove. Letting the horse have its head, he sprinted for the trees, crouching and zigzagging through the tall grass. Not until he reached the safety of the grove did he reach for his Colt and realize he hadn't worn it.

He had a Winchester in a saddle boot, but to reach it he'd have to leave the cover and get to the horse. Cursing under his breath, he ducked from tree to tree until he was right in front of the bay, as close as he could get with cover and still a good thirty feet away.

But he had to have the gun.

CHAPTER 15

Morgan shucked his hat and tunneled through the grass, hoping to God the shooter was not looking down on him from any height. The bay was nervous, and skittered to one side, shaking its mane and dancing away. He grasped for the reins, felt them slide through his fingers as they closed, leaving him with a fistful of grass.

Like Tantalus, he tried again, moving more slowly and talking to the horse in a soothing baritone. Once again, he could just reach the reins and this time he lunged, twisting his hand and rolling to wrap the reins around him as the horse shied once more. He held the reins and tugged them down, talking to the horse more loudly.

The bay calmed down a little, but still wanted to dance away as Morgan got to his knees. The horse was between him and the shooter now, and he got into a crouch, patting the bay's neck and almost hugging him as he reached for the Winchester. A shot pinged off his saddle, and the horse reared up, nearly knocking Morgan off his feet.

He calmed the horse again, closing his hands over the rifle butt, and started to slide it out. His eye caught the groove burrowed across the seat of the saddle where the leather had been deeply plowed, and he cursed under his breath. Jerking the Winchester free, he tried to remember how many shells he had in the magazine, then, wanting to take no chances, slipped along the bay's flank and unlashed his saddlebags. He had to jerk them free, because his ammunition was on the other side and there was no time to waste trying to slip around behind the bay or maneuver it around like a drunken show horse.

When the bags came free, Morgan dug in his heels and started to drag the horse by main force toward the cottonwood grove. Another shot sailed overhead, its whine suddenly expiring as it slammed into a tree. He heard the clap of the gunshot, a little closer than the first few.

Morgan scanned the terrain as best he could, trying to keep from falling and keep the horse moving at the same time. There wasn't a sign of the shooter's location. Now he was beginning to wonder if there might not be two men. Either that, or the shooter was closing on him quicker than he thought.

He got the bay into the trees, pulled it into a thick clump of underbrush, and tied it off. Opening the saddlebags, he pulled out a box of ammunition, stuffed half the box into his pocket, and shoved the box back into the bag. On a dead run, he cut toward the end of the grove. The shooter couldn't possibly see him now, and he wanted to get into a position to see where the gunman was before he decided what to do.

In the back of his mind was the nagging thought that it had to be Kinkaid. The marshal knew where he was. And no one else knew him well enough to give a damn. The only run-in he'd had in Cross Creek was with Deak Slayton, and Slayton was already in the ground. Or did Slayton have friends, someone who might hold Morgan responsible for what had happened to the cowhand?

If he could get a look at the shooter, he'd have an idea. But the troubling thing was that if it should turn out to be one of Slayton's saddle buddies, he couldn't tell Kinkaid. And he couldn't shoot the gunman without giving Kinkaid an excuse to come after him. Morgan was in a corner, and the walls were damn thick.

There hadn't been a shot in quite a while. He knelt behind the last thick cottonwood and pushed some underbrush aside. Watching the grass for any unnatural movement, he swept his eyes back and forth across the meadow, starting in close and gradually widening the sweep as he looked out across the open field.

There was a slight breeze, and it made the tall grass ripple like the surface of a lake. The blossoms of the paintbrush and lupine and columbine bent before the wind, then snapped back. They were

thicker stemmed than the grass and it took more
to bend them, so he concentrated on them.

He could hear the sighing of the wind as it slid
across the surface of the grass, almost like dry sand
running off the blade of a shovel. And there was a
steady droning he didn't place at first. He bent lower
and finally realized what it was. Skimming just over
the tops of the grass, bees by the thousands, their
buzzing blending into a single, steady roar, filled
the meadow with sound.

Suddenly, a big jackrabbit, its ears bobbing as
it hopped, zigzagged toward him as if something
had spooked it. He backtracked as best he could,
but the ten or fifteen yards he'd seen of the jackrabbit's flight vanished in motionless grass. But
something had frightened it. If not the gunman,
what could it have been?

Then a cloud of bees suddenly erupted, like
smoke rising on heated air. For a moment, it looked
almost like brown snow climbing back to the heavens, then it settled slowly back to earth. He waited,
hoping to see another cloud, but nothing happened.
If there was someone out there, someone who had
spooked the jackrabbit and aggravated the swarm
of bees, he had stopped moving.

For a minute, he thought about dropping one
or two shots into the area, letting the Winchester
slugs tunnel through the grass on the off chance he
might hit, or at least frighten, his so-far-unseen as-
sailant. But he didn't really want to shoot anybody,
even Kinkaid, if he could avoid it. He was on the
edge of being able to put that all behind him. If he
shot Kinkaid, a man who himself had been going

out of his way to call attention to himself, it would be an open invitation to others.

And if it wasn't Kinkaid, he wanted to know who it was. Maybe he could talk the shooter out of whatever stupidity had pushed him to try and back-shoot a man he couldn't even know.

Then a third possibility hit him. Suppose Kinkaid, or Kinkaid's inquiry, had gotten around. Suppose some other misguided glory-seeking sonofabitch had come to Cross Creek for the same reason Kinkaid had begun to push and pull him, trying to ruffle his feathers? It was remote, but possible. Hell, anything was possible when you'd lived the life Morgan Atwater had, whether by choice or stupidity, had the misfortune to lead.

Then a second cloud of bees erupted, thousands of dark specks, their transparent wings catching the light and flashing like tiny beacons, the light immediately all but absorbed by the dark, furry little bodies. There *was* something out there.

Morgan tucked his head down and started forward on his hands and knees. When he reached the grass, he lay flat, reaching out with the muzzle of the Winchester and pushing the grass aside as far into the meadow as he could reach.

When he saw nothing, he listened for some disturbance of the grass. Under the constant ebb and flow of the wind, the blades scraped against one another, the rattle of millions of tiny swords. He heard nothing for a long time, but refused to believe there was no one there. Whoever had tried so hard to kill him would not have abruptly abandoned the attack without even a single shot fired in reply. The gunman had to be out there.

He heard the bay nicker, once, then again. He swiveled his head, but couldn't see his mount. Backing on his hands and knees, he moved into the trees again and got warily to his feet.

The horse nickered again, but he still couldn't see it. Sprinting through the trees, he heard footsteps for a second, stopped, and heard them vanish. They were not his own. He was convinced of that. Racing again toward his mount, he broke into a small clearing. Morgan caught a glimpse of the bay and, when he angled to the right, beyond the horse, the head and shoulders of a retreating figure.

The hat was a nondescript gray Stetson, and he tried to remember what Kinkaid had been wearing. He remembered the marshal's hat was light, but wasn't sure it was the same color. He heard a horse whinny, then hoofbeats as he charged on toward the bay. When he reached the horse, he shouted in rage. His saddle lay on the ground, the cinch neatly sliced through.

Sprinting toward the sound of the hoofbeats, he reached the far edge of the grove in time to see a horse and rider reach the crest of the hill. He still didn't get a good enough look when the man broke over the hill and down out of sight. The horseman, presumably the same man who had fired on him, was wearing a shirt but no jacket. He'd never seen Kinkaid without one. That morning, he had been wearing a shiny black coat over a blue shirt. The fleeing man's shirt was also blue, but blue shirts were a dime a dozen.

He hadn't seen enough to be sure of anything.

In his heart he wanted to believe it was Kinkaid, but he knew that was only because he didn't want to live with yet another uncertainty dogging his footsteps. Kinkaid's machinations he could live with, if he had to, and guard against because he knew the source.

But if there was another man who wanted him dead, a man he didn't know, perhaps had never seen, then he wasn't safe from anyone *but* Kinkaid. You can't guard against assault from a shadow, you can't protect yourself from being shot in the back by any man who might just happen to be behind you.

Cursing aloud, his voice getting bolder and more furious as he stomped toward the bay, he raged until he felt his voice crack, his throat grow raw. Panting, he sat down with his back against a cottonwood, kicked out at the useless saddle, and shook his head in complete frustration.

He cradled the Winchester across his knees, then remembering he'd tossed his hat aside, he got up to find it. Making his way back toward the edge of the grove, he heard rapid hoofbeats approaching. Morgan hunkered down behind a clump of laurel. The hoofbeats slowed, then stopped.

He could hear a voice shouting, but he couldn't make out the words. He levered a shell into the chamber of the Winchester and held his breath. The hoofbeats had come from the opposite direction, so it couldn't have been the man he'd seen riding away. Maybe he'd been right after all. Maybe there had been two men.

The voice was drifting away now, and he heard

the uncertainty in it. The newcomer was drifting along the front of the grove, moving away from him. Cutting back through the brush, he tried to close the gap. If the man was moving cautiously enough, he might be able to slip up behind him. With the element of surprise, he might not have to shoot.

Again, the voice shouted, but he still couldn't make out the words. Morgan moved out past the trees and sprinted through the grass. He could see the top of a hat now, and he crossed his fingers. He was a hundred and fifty yards away, maybe a little more, but the gap was narrowing. The man on horseback was paying more attention to his search than to the possibility that someone might be hunting him. Either dumb or careless. Maybe both.

But you never threw away a break like that. Not when your life depended on it. And there was no doubt in Morgan's mind that was the case.

He could see the man's shoulders now, and something about the shirt looked familiar. Not Kinkaid, he was sure of that. But who, then?

The man shouted again, then stood in the stirrups, his hands cupped around his mouth as he shouted once more.

Morgan charged ahead. The man must have heard something because he started to turn. Morgan had closed to under a hundred yards as the man's horse kicked sidewise, cantering downhill a few yards, and the horseman sat down after almost falling from his mount.

At fifty yards, Morgan stopped. It was something about the man, the set of his shoulders from behind. And that shirt. Then the man yelled again. And this time Morgan could understand it. "Dad...? Dad...?"

It was Tom.

What the hell was he doing out here?

"Tom," Morgan shouted.

Startled out of his wits, Tom turned, his mouth a huge, vacant "O" of surprise.

"What the hell are you doing?"

Tom climbed out of the saddle. "Are you alright?" he asked. "I was out hunting, and I heard gunshots. I thought maybe that man...Mother told me about him, the marshal, and I thought..."

"I'm alright."

"Somebody just tried to kill you, didn't he?"

Morgan nodded. "Looks like. Did a job on my saddle, too, to make sure I couldn't catch up with him, once he realized he wasn't going to get me."

"Who was it?"

"I don't know, Tom."

"Is this what it's like?"

"'Fraid so."

"And that's why you left."

Morgan didn't answer. He didn't have to, because it wasn't really a question.

CHAPTER 16

Mondays were always busy at Lyle Henessey's store. People took Sundays off. Part of the time they spent in church. The rest of it, they spent realizing what they were short on or just plain out of. Everybody had the same idea. Get there early to get the best pick. And when the Monday in question was the first Monday of the month, the rush paled only in comparison to 'forty-nine.

Moving freight across half a continent tended to brutalize it just a little. Nails got a little rusty. Soap turned a bit rancid. The knives got dull and the bullets tended to run a yard or two short or high and to the left. Nothing, it seemed, was as hardy as the people themselves. And when you had one store to shop in, you damn sure wanted to get the pick of a decidedly uncertain litter.

By ten o'clock, Henessey was breathing heavily, as much draped across his counter as leaning on it. Morgan was younger, but he was less experienced. It was doubly hard on him, and left him little more than a limp copy of his employer. The pace started to slacken around eleven, and at eleven-thirty, Henessey felt reasonably sure of a lull to wander off for a beer and fresh rainbow trout at the The Hangin' Tree Hotel's restaurant.

As he walked out the door, he told Morgan he'd be back by twelve-thirty, when it would be his turn for lunch. It sounded more like wishful thinking than a promise he had any chance of keeping. As the customer traffic diminished still further, Morgan was starting to pace himself, saving what little energy he had left to chew his noon meal.

It was ten after twelve before the store was devoid of customers for the first time since Henessey had turned the key in the lock at seven o'clock.

Morgan dropped into a rough chair crudely fashioned from a nail keg and four two-by-fours. It wasn't comfortable, but it held him up and for that he was as grateful as he had the energy to be.

His eyes were starting to droop. He felt like he hadn't slept in a week. Most people bought in bulk, and that meant hefting most things by the sack or the barrel. He was only dimly aware that the tinkling bell was someone opening the door. He felt a little puff of hot air blowing in from the street. He knew he should open his eyes, but he was too damned tired to care.

He thought it might be Lyle, and started to open his eyes, or at least struggle to keep them from slamming shut like a pair of matching mausoleums. He felt a hand on his shoulder then, and turned his head in slow motion.

It wasn't Lyle. It was Tom.

"Dad," he said. The word sounded strange on his lips, and it was plain that he was just as aware of the novelty as Morgan was.

Bolting upright, Morgan rubbed his tired eyes. "Tom, what are you doing here?"

Tom popped a folded piece of paper from his shirt pocket. Morgan looked at him more closely, forcing his eyes artificially wide, trying to look alert and in command. He noticed the sweat stains down the center of Tom's shirt, the dark semicircles under each arm. "Hot out there," he said.

Tom nodded, then flicked the paper with a thumbnail. "Supply day," he said.

"How come so late? Most of the people around here seem to get up in time to watch creation."

"Yeah, well, it's a small place, but the workload isn't. I had a few things to do. Mom wanted to come herself, but I thought I ought to."

"You didn't tell her about what happened yesterday, did you?"

"No. I had to tell her why you needed the spare saddle, so I made something up. I think she bought it, but I'm not sure."

"What'd you tell her? I don't want to give it away, in case the subject comes up."

"Told her a stirrup broke."

"She didn't ask how come I couldn't ride with just one?"

"Didn't give her a chance to."

"Well, listen, don't go getting any fool notions, now. We don't know what happened, not really. Not either one of us."

"You don't, maybe, but I got a pretty good idea."

"Yeah, how's that?"

"I went to school with Deak Slayton's brother Tyler. Seems like if you put two and two together, you come up with Kinkaid. I do, anyhow."

Morgan nodded. "Me too, but I don't think I can do anything with it. Or about it."

"I know." Tom fell silent. He stared at the shopping list, looked around the store for a couple of small items, and, when he spotted them, brought them back to the counter. There was something on his mind, but Morgan was going to stand back and let him get to it in his own way. When he was ready. There was no percentage in pressing too hard. It seemed like the less pressure Morgan brought to bear, the better his results were likely to be.

When it was no longer possible to delay, Tom sat down on the counter, kicking his boots against the front panel like an anxious four-year-old. The drumming sound of his heels on the hollow front was the only sound in the store for a long moment. "See," Tom finally said.

Morgan waited.

When Tom didn't go any further, he asked, "See what?"

"I been thinking."

"Oh?"

"Yeah. I wasn't exactly fair to you when you first got here. I..."

"Don't worry about it, Tom. It's not..."

"No, let me finish. I messed it up and I got to set it right. The best way I know how." He looked at his father through hooded eyes. "We got a lot of catching up to do, just like you said. I almost didn't give you the chance, but that's all finished with. I don't want to see anything get in the way, now. Or anybody."

"Son, there's nothing you can do about it."

"There should be."

"You're right. There should be, but there isn't. See, ordinarily, when something like this happens, you can go one of two ways. You can go to your gun and handle it yourself, or you can go to the law, which anyway is almost the same thing, because the law isn't really much more than a better gun than you can shoot yourself. But where do you go when the law is the problem, rather than the solution?"

"It isn't fair, though."

"Life isn't fair. Wait a minute, I take that back. That's too damn easy. Sometimes we make it impossible for life to be fair. The things we do, they ripple, and you can't control that. You throw a rock in the water, there's gonna be some ripples. You throw two or three or four in, all those ripples interfere with one another, they connect up in funny ways, they change each other, and those changes change things somewhere when they collide. What I did, Tom, and there's no two ways about it, I threw a whole damn pocketful of rocks into the pond. All I can do now is wait until the water settles down again."

"But that was so long ago."

"Sure, it was a long time ago. But that doesn't make any difference. All those ripples are still out there spreading further and further. I can't even see 'em anymore. But I know they're there. And I know that Brett Kinkaid is just one of 'em. And maybe not the worst. The thing that sticks in my craw is that that's all he is, a goddamned ripple. And I made it myself. I made Brett Kinkaid. It's my fault, no two ways about it."

"Still . . ."

The bell tinkled again before Tom could finish his objection. Morgan looked up, but he didn't really have to. He knew who it would be.

He wasn't wrong.

"How's the storekeeper today," Kinkaid asked. He laughed, a phlegmy sound more like something was caught in his throat than an expression of amusement. "You gonna lose your hand and your eye, you keep pushing pins and flour, Morgan. That's no way for a man like you to earn a living."

"It'll do," Atwater said.

"Oh, Morgan, *Morg*an, you're selling yourself short, that's what you're selling. What's the matter with you, lost your nerve?"

Morgan took a deep breath. "You need something, Marshal?"

"Surely do, Morgan. I surely do. Need me some more of them Remington Arms .45s. Hope you got some in stock. See, I been practicing a whole lot. My hand's got blisters on it, I been practicing so much."

"Maybe you ought to find some other way to enforce the law, Mr. Kinkaid."

"Now, see, that's where you're wrong, Morgan. There *is* no other way to enforce the law. Cowpokes and hard cases, they don't understand no other way. You ought to know that. Or has it been so long that you can't even remember what it was like?"

"I remember."

"Do you, now? Do you remember that last few seconds, just before you draw your gun? Remember that funny feeling on the back of your neck? Hell, I can feel the hair on my arms rise up. Almost like I could count 'em. I hear my heart beating in my ears. Ba-boom. Ba-boom. And you notice things about the other guy, too. You see his eyes get real wide. Sometimes, an eye jumps a little, a little throbbing thing is there in one cheek, like a chick peckin' at a shell, maybe. But I see it all real plain."

"You're welcome to see whatever the hell you want." Morgan slapped a box of shells on the counter. "Dollar fifteen," he said.

"Can I run a tab, Morgan? Seems like I use so many of these things, I just might be keepin' Henessey afloat." He picked up the box of bullets and hefted it, like a man appraising a large jewel he suspects might be flawed in some way, but which is so large he can't refuse to admire it.

"You'll have to talk to Mr. Henessey about that."

"What if I just stick this here box in my pocket and walk out? What would you do then, Morgan? Call the marshal?" He laughed that same strangled laugh.

"I guess Mr. Henessey would have your pay attached."

"Would he do that to me?"

It was Morgan's turn to laugh. "I can't think of any reason why not, Mr. Kinkaid. Deadbeats generally get what's coming to them. Even in Cross Creek."

"Oh, yes, Morgan. All sorts of folks get what's, coming to them. Especially in Cross Creek. You can bank on that." He fished the money out of his pocket and slapped it on the counter. "You surely can."

He finally turned to Tom. "This must be your boy," he said. "He kinda favors you."

Morgan didn't respond, and Tom stared blankly at the marshal, his face flat as a shovel, and just as steely.

"Nice family you got, Morgan. Pretty little lady, the missus is. You tell her I said hello again, would you?"

"I don't think so."

"Just being friendly, is all. A man's got to be friendly with his neighbors. Especially when he knows he gonna be seein' a lot of them."

"You finished, or can I get you something else, Kinkaid?"

"Finished? Why, no, Morgan, I'm not. Hardiy begun, to tell the truth." He tucked the box of ammunition in his pocket, then tapped it through the cloth. "Don't run out of these, now." He nodded at Tom, flipped Morgan that same snotty salute, and walked out.

Tom stared at his father, but he didn't know what to say.

"Forget it, Tom," Morgan said. "He's all smoke."

"Gunsmoke, maybe."

CHAPTER 17

"I'll be back in a while, Dad." He walked across the street and Morgan watched him go. Each time he lost sight of Tom, it was like losing him all over again. He was sensitive, maybe too sensitive, to how much of his life had been spent without the boy and, worse, how much of the boy's life had been spent without him.

To himself, he whispered, "I've got to stop thinking of him as a boy. Katie was right. He's all grown up. He can't ever really be my son, but I hope he can become my friend."

When Tom stepped through the door of the dry goods shop across the street, it was as if he had turned a page in a book. One chapter had ended and the next had not yet begun. He stared after the dim, open space where Tom had been a few seconds before. He couldn't decide whether he was looking at a new void in his life or the return of that emptiness that had been there for so long. He rubbed his lips with one hand, then turned back to his work.

Packing Tom's order, he kept thinking about Brett Kinkaid. He had to find some way to close that particular book altogether. He didn't want to run, had done enough running, really. He knew that what he had been running from was not so much his past as it was himself. No way in hell he could outrun that particular fury. What he had to do was to become someone else entirely, change himself so completely that he would seem to be someone else not only to others but to the man who stared into his shaving mirror every morning.

A tall order.

In the back room, a sack of beans draped over his shoulder, Morgan was clinging to a ladder when he heard the first scream. A piercing shriek, it sounded more like a bird cry than a human voice, a screaming eagle, or an angry hawk. He shrugged it off, even when a deeper voice responded. Neither was intelligible, and he was getting curious. By the time he reached the floor, a full-blown argument was in progress. A man and a woman venting some inexpressible spleen, maybe the ultimate war between the genders.

Probably sex somewhere in the bottom of that barrel, he thought, as he dropped the beans on a sack of flour. The bottom sack cushioned the blow and spewed a great cloud of powdery dust. Morgan coughed, and clapped his hands free of the flour residue as he walked to the door.

Already he could see a crowd gathering in the street. The men were laughing, the women talking among themselves and pretending not to look. When he reached the doorway, he saw the antagonists. A woman in a slip and bare feet stood on the open second-floor porch of The Hangin' Tree Hotel. My hotel, he thought. She was gesticulating at a cowhand in the street, who kept shaking his head, pointing and shouting something in no language Morgan had ever heard. But he understood it, all the same.

People were beginning to treat the argument like a theatrical performance, even clapping after a particularly histrionic exchange. As near as anyone could make out, the woman, whose name apparently was Marlene, felt she was entitled to compensation for certain services of an intimate nature she had rendered to the cowhand. For his part, the cowhand, a man known only as McKay, refused to pay on the grounds of incompetence in the delivery of said services.

As the nature of the dispute became more widely appreciated, the men laughed louder, and the women started to drift away. The latter talked among themselves, raising their own voices to drown out the argument.

Morgan leaned against the roof column to the left of the door. He spotted Henessey in the crowd, who saw him and waved, a grin splitting his face into unequal portions from ear to ear. He gestured for Morgan to join him, but Morgan refused.

He was getting ready to go on back inside when he spotted Brett Kinkaid leaning out of the marshal's office door.

Morgan cupped his hands and shouted, "Lyle, shut him up, quick."

Henessey turned. It was obvious he hadn't understood and Morgan started off the porch, pointing down the street toward Kinkaid, who was outside now, standing with hands on hips and shaking his head.

Henessey got the point at once, and bullied his way through the crowd. Draping an arm around McKay, he tried to drag the cowboy away, but it only seemed to heighten the intensity of his passion. McKay broke free, turned long enough to plant a stiff arm, with open palm, in the middle of Lyle's chest and shove him away. The crowd parted like waves around the prow of a ship, then closed again as Lyle stumbled and fell at the rear of the throng.

Morgan stepped off the boardwalk as Kinkaid started up the street. Henessey was struggling back through the crowd again, but no one but Morgan and Lyle seemed to realize what was about to happen, what would certainly happen unless someone could shut McKay up and get him off the street. Even then, Morgan knew, it might be difficult to convince Kinkaid to let it alone. But if McKay was still shouting when the marshal reached him, it would be altogether impossible.

Henessey managed to break through the front edge of the milling circle. Morgan was at the back of the crowd now. Lyle snaked a thick arm around McKay's neck and yanked him backward. The cowboy turned again and caught Henessey on the jaw with an uppercut that staggered the older man and sent him reeling. Marlene shrieked even louder, whether for Henessey to mind his own business or for McKay to leave the storekeeper alone wasn't clear.

The words "leave him alone" hung in the air, but no one except Marlene seemed to know to whom they referred and to whom they had been addressed. McKay didn't care. Glad to have an adversary he could deal with on more familiar and more direct terms, he swung at Henessey again. He bore in with his arms flailing, but he was three sheets to the wind and the punches sailed harmlessly wide as Henessey charged forward with his head lowered.

McKay tripped and fell and Henessey, too much a gentleman to press his advantage, stood circling until a boot caught him in the groin and he doubled over and fell to his knees, vomiting all over McKay's legs.

Morgan broke through the crowd and hauled Henessey out of reach of another kick. He had his back to the cowboy when something caught him on the side of the head. He went down hard, and realized McKay had cracked him with his pistol barrel. Morgan lay there staring up at the blue sky, his head spinning. He was aware of a warm trickle down the side of his head, the sticky moisture puddling in his right ear.

Then everything went black.

Kinkaid was at the back of the crowd now, and the men started to back away as he shoved on through. McKay, still blissfully unaware of the marshal's arrival, and geared up enough that he might not have cared if he had known, tucked his gun away and turned back to his original adversary. Marlene had a better vantage point, and she stood with her knuckles crammed between her painted lips.

It finally dawned on McKay that something was wrong. He whirled in a circle once, then again before his eyes lit on Kinkaid. He was drunk, but not so drunk he couldn't realize he had dug himself a very deep hole. The marshal walked past the cowboy and stood under the porch of the hotel. He pointed at Marlene and told her to go inside.

Tom Atwater was stepping out of the dry goods store next door to the hotel as Kinkaid pulled his shiny silk jacket back off his hip. He saw Morgan on the ground, Henessey bent over him, and Kinkaid walking toward McKay. The cowboy unbuckled his gunbelt and let it fall as Kinkaid took another step and then another.

"You going to regret that, boy," the marshal said.

"I don't want no trouble, Marshal," McKay said. He dropped his gun in the dirt, then backed away, holding his arms out as if to ward off the menace approaching him.

"Too late for that, boy. Trouble already arrived. You're lookin' at him."

"Leave him alone, Kinkaid," Henessey shouted. "He dropped his gun. Just lock him up until he's sober."

"Henessey, you are fat and you are an old man. I don't need any advice from a shopkeeper," he said. Then turning to McKay, "Pick it up, boy."

"No, sir."

"Pick it up. You brought it to town, use the damn thing."

"No, sir, I won't do that."

"You might as well, boy."

McKay hesitated. He started to bend.

"Don't do it!" Henessey shouted. "He'll kill you."

McKay looked at him. His light blue eyes looked like two huge cornflowers. They bugged out of his face, and beads of sweat coalesced on his forehead and ran down into them. He blinked, trying to unblur his vision as he stared at Henessey, then at the gun and finally at Marshal Kinkaid.

"Pick it up!"

McKay licked his lips and started to bend again.

Tom saw the movement and he saw Kinkaid's fingers uncurl. He launched himself through the air as McKay backed up a step and Kinkaid lowered his hand toward the Colt on his hip. Tom hit him just above the kidneys, driving a shoulder in hard and sending Kinkaid sprawling.

The marshal cursed as he sprawled in the dust. He sat up as Tom got to his feet. He looked up at the young man and his lips curled back in a smile. "Well, well, well," he said. "Son, you have just bought yourself a world of trouble."

Kinkaid climbed to his feet and brushed the yellow dust from his jacket. "Looks like you're gonna get to see the inside of our little jail, Atwater."

Morgan groaned and tried to sit up. Henessey was bent over him trying to wake him up, but Morgan was only dimly aware of what was going on. He shook his head and braced himself on Henessey's shoulder. But his head was spinning and he fell back in the dirt as Kinkaid pulled his gun.

Henessey heard the scrape of metal on leather and leaped to his feet. He grabbed Kinkaid by the arm and said, "Leave him be, Kinkaid. All he did was stop you from killing an unarmed man. You may be the law in Cross Creek, but that ain't a crime, and you ain't gonna *be* the law much longer."

Kinkaid smiled. "You got to work that out with Tate Crimmins, Lyle. You know that," he said. Gesturing with his gun, he directed Tom to walk to his office.

"You hurt that boy and I'll see you pay for it, Kinkaid."

The marshal didn't even bother to glance over his shoulder.

Henessey worked feverishly to rouse Morgan, and when he couldn't, grabbed a couple of men and brought him into the store. He moistened a towel in the horse trough in the alley beside his store and after a few minutes, Morgan regained consciousness.

He was only vaguely aware of where he was, but he knew by the look on Henessey's face that something was wrong. As his head cleared, he remembered seeing Tom step out of the doorway of the dry goods shop, and he remembered seeing Kinkaid push through the crowd.

"Dammit, Morgan, wake up." Henessey screamed it at him, and he jerked his head away, aggravating the already severe headache that threatened to split his skull in two.

"Kinkaid's got Tom," he said. "We got to go get him out of jail."

"Help me up, Lyle, dammit. Help me up." Morgan got to his feet and went down on one knee almost immediately.

"You come as soon as you can. I got to get down there," Henessey said.

CHAPTER 18

As Tom was pushed toward the jail, prodded in the back by Kinkaid's gun barrel, he kept glancing over his shoulder. The crowd seemed confused by what was happening. McKay stood on the front edge, holding his face in his hands and shaking. Some of the others took a few tentative steps after the marshal and his prisoner, but Kinkaid whirled on them, waved the pistol, and shouted, "You all go home."

He pointed the big Colt first at one, then another, and then a third. No one wanted to die. And no one on the street, least of all Tom Atwater, doubted that Kinkaid would shoot. The marshal was very close to the edge, and a single footstep might send him over the edge. If he went, and everyone seemed to understand this, he would drag others with him. He couldn't kill them all, they knew that, but no one wanted to be the first.

Tom was looking for Morgan. He had lost sight of him as he went down, and never did see him again. Then, when Henessey bulled his way through the crowd, Tom saw Morgan's limp body suspended like a side of beef and he stopped. Kinkaid saw it and he turned.

When he turned back, he smiled. "Your old man don't look so high and mighty now, does he?"

Tom stared at him, and Kinkaid stuck his face forward, "Does he?" There was some indescribable hatred in Kinkaid and it was reflected in every muscle and sinew and tendon. It was as if a human skin had been shed and something venomous and ugly had been born.

Knowing what Kinkaid wanted to hear, he shook his head gently. "No," he said, "he doesn't."

"Funny, ain't it, how he come back here and I come here, and now lookit what's happened. We are gonna have to settle this, you know. Me and him." Kinkaid shook his head, as if in amazement. "We surely are gonna have to settle it. Almost enough to give a man religion, you know that?"

Tom couldn't help himself. "Religion? You must be joking."

Kinkaid lashed out with the pistol. The gun caught Tom on the cheek under the left eye, and the lead sight opened a gash an inch long. He fell to his knees, but wouldn't give Kinkaid the satisfaction of reaching up to touch the wound.

"Get up!"

Tom struggled to his feet. He stumbled and fell, then got up again. Kinkaid kicked him and Tom rolled over, then scrambled to his feet. He started to charge Kinkaid, saw the gun, and looked into the black hole of the barrel. He was trembling. He wanted to kill Kinkaid, and wanted to run as far and as fast as he could.

But he could do neither. Again he looked up the street. The crowd had thinned, and the handful of onlookers just stood mute as statues staring after the marshal.

"Don't be lookin' for help, Atwater," Kinkaid said. "There ain't no help. You think anybody in this shithole of a town is going to come and save you? No way."

He poked Tom in the ribs with the gun, and for one rapturous second, Tom saw himself grabbing the gun and turning it on his tormentor. But it would never work. And he thought of his mother. Who would help her? Morgan? Maybe, and if Kinkaid killed him, then what?

He stumbled backward toward the jail. Every couple of steps he felt the hard barrel of the Colt slam into his spine. It was like Kinkaid *wanted* him to run, or to strike back. At the entrance to the marshal's office, Kinkaid brought the barrel down hard on Tom's shoulders. Something cracked, like a dry branch snapping off, and searing pain flashed all through the shoulder. His arm went limp.

"Up, watch your step, sonny boy. Don't want you to get hurt." Kinkaid laughed, shoving him toward the boardwalk. He missed the step and fell, rolling his body to the side to avoid landing on the injured shoulder. The impact was enough. He cried out and rolled onto his back. Kinkaid grabbed him by the bad arm and pulled him to his feet. Tom thought the arm was coming off, it hurt so much.

Kinkaid shoved him through the door, and his shoulder slammed into the door frame. He bounced off, and a wave of white light washed over him. He couldn't see anymore, and he couldn't hear. All he could do was feel, and the pain was everything. He staggered into the office blinking his eyes, one hand, the right, partly extended for obstacles he couldn't see, the other curled protectively over his broken collarbone.

The white light gradually disappeared, and he could see the office, materializing out of the brilliant void like a photograph he had once seen developed in Warren Brewster's newspaper office. But seeing things didn't change them.

Kinkaid shoved him into the cell block, then kicked him in the lower back. The impact sent him spinning and he crashed into the stone wall at the far end and slipped to the floor. Kinkaid opened the last cell door, then holstered his Colt. He grabbed Tom under the arms and hauled him into the cell.

"Get up, you little bastard," he screamed. "Get up!"

Tom reached out for support, grabbed the pallet-mattressed cot and was halfway up when Kinkaid kicked him again. This one broke his nose and he went down and lay there, afraid to move. He heard the cell door slam, then the heavy jangle of a key ring. When the key ground in the lock, he knew it was only going to get worse, a lot worse, before it got a little better.

He was bleeding from the gash on his face and from his broken nose. The pain was so intense he couldn't stand the thought of movement. But he had to. He crawled up onto the cot, using his one good arm, and rolled onto his back. Covering his eyes with one hand, he felt his consciousness slipping away.

And he was thankful.

Kinkaid stood in the cell-block doorway, his back to the office, and watched Tom for a few minutes. It won't be long now, he thought. He can't overlook this. Aloud, he said, "Mr. Morgan Atwater, we are about to get our business done. Yessiree, we are about to get our business done."

He backed through the doorway, still staring at Tom's motionless form, and closed the door. Conscious of his role, he sat behind his desk, but had difficulty arranging his limbs comfortably. They seemed to have lives of their own. One leg kept jumping, his toe patting the floor irregularly. He looked at the leg, willing it to stop and, when it refused, pushed down on it with his right hand.

His left hand lay on the desk, its fingers wriggling like spider legs as he drummed the wood with his fingertips. He sucked his teeth and stared at the front door. Sooner or later, he knew, someone would come through that door. He hoped it would be Morgan Atwater. He had to come, now. And if not, well, he still had the bait. He would come, sooner or later.

He was watching the sunlit strip of dirt in the naked street, expecting a shadow, something, some warning that the last stage was about to begin. But when the shadow appeared, it was not Morgan Atwater's. It was too bulky for that, too rounded, like an oil stain in the dust.

Then he saw Lyle Henessey's fat face peer around the corner. He didn't look happy, but that was alright. He didn't really give a damn what Lyle Henessey thought. The burly storekeeper stepped into the office, his bulk filling the doorway.

"Where's Tommy Atwater?" Henessey asked.

Here it comes, Kinkaid thought. He leaned back in the chair and propped his booted feet on the desk. The chair creaked while he decided what to say.

"You heard me," Henessey demanded. "Where is he?"

"Who wants to know?"

"I do. I'm here, and I'm asking. I want to know."

"Not his father? His father don't give a damn? Seems unnatural."

"Damn you, Kinkaid, where is he? I want to see him."

"He's in back. In jail. Where he belongs. Don't think he's up to visitors, though. Hell, I'm not sure criminals ought to have visitors in the first place."

"That boy don't belong in jail, Kinkaid. He didn't do anything."

"The hell he didn't. Jumped me when my back was turned. Stopped me from doing my job. That's against the law."

"There is no law here. You stopped doing your

job a long time ago. Now, let him go."

Kinkaid shook his head. "Can't do it, Lyle."

"You'd better."

"Or what? What happens if I don't let him go, Lyle? You going to make me? Is that it?"

"Your days in Cross Creek are about up, Kinkaid. We already sent a telegram to the capital. You can leave now and go on your way, or you can wait around for the federal marshal to take you away. Either way, you're gone. And I don't give a good goddamn which way it is."

"Maybe I'll just wait for the marshal. In the meantime, I might have a little talk with Mr. Crimmins."

"Tate Crimmins won't help you, Kinkaid. He sent the damned telegram."

"I think I'll wait for him to tell me that. We got to discuss my compensation. After all, I have a contract, and honorable men got to honor pieces of paper like that, don't they?"

"You wouldn't know an honorable man from a diamondback. Where's Tommy?"

Kinkaid jerked a finger toward the cell-block doorway. "He's in there, like I told you. You can visit with him if you like, but you ain't taking him. Not now. Not yet."

"Give me the key."

"It ain't locked. You can go in."

Henessey stomped to the door and pulled it open. He moved down the cellblock and stood in front of Tom's cell. He tried the door, but it was locked. He saw the blood, and he called to Tom, who hadn't moved, "Tommy, you alright, boy? Tommy? It's me, Lyle Henessey. You alright?"

When he still got no answer, he curled his big hands around the bars and tried to pull the door open. It didn't budge, and he slammed a fist into the lock-plate in frustration. He ran back to the office.

"What did you do to that boy?"

"He was resisting arrest. I persuaded him it wasn't a good idea." Kinkaid laughed. "Took some persuading, too, he did."

"I know what you're doing, Kinkaid."

The marshal shook his head, rocking slightly in the chair. He lowered his feet to the floor, tilted his hat back, and smiled into Henessey's face. "I do too, Lyle. I do too."

"You won't get away with this."

"Think not? Well, then, maybe the kindly folk of Cross Creek don't want law and order after all. Maybe they just want to whine and snivel. Afraid of a bunch of drunken cowboys, that what it was, Lyle? All you big men bring in a whip to keep the little boys in line?"

"You're mad, Kinkaid."

"Not mad, just real good at my job. And I guess you got to be a little crazy in this business. I mean, it is more dangerous than selling beans and mucilage, Lyle. Of course, if you got somebody better in mind, well, then maybe we should just see if he's up to snuff."

"I know what you're doing. And I know why."

"That makes two of us, Lyle."

"I'm warning you, Kinkaid, anything happens to that boy, you'll have to answer for it."

"I got nothing but answers, Lyle. You ought to know that. Buy 'em by the box in your store."

CHAPTER 19

Morgan was sitting up when Henessey stormed in. He knew the news was bad, and he slipped down off the counter. His head throbbed and he felt with his fingertips for the painful lump on the back of his skull. "Where's Tom?" he asked.

"He's in jail, Morgan. And he's been beat up pretty bad."

Morgan started for the door, but Henessey blocked his path. "Where you think you're going?"

"To get my gun."

"No you ain't, Morgan. That's just what Kinkaid wants. You know it and I know it. But you ain't in no shape to lock horns with that bastard. We got to do this carefully."

"You do. I don't. I'm not a careful man, Lyle."

"You are now, whether you like it or not. We'll

do this one by the book. And we'll do it right."

Morgan tried to brush past him, but Henessey locked him in a bear hug. He dragged the struggling man back toward the storeroom. Morgan was still groggy, and Henessey was a big, powerful man. He might not have been in the best of shape, but in his weakened condition, Morgan was still no match for him.

Henessey shoved him into the storeroom and closed the door. He dropped the lock bar in place, then turned to the two men in the store. "Ben," he said, "go get Tate Crimmins. You get him here and you get him here fast. I don't give a damn what he's doing. I don't care if he's foreclosing on a mortgage, you get him."

Ben nodded once, tried not to look dubious, and shook his head more vigorously.

"What the hell you waiting for, Ben?" Henessey shouted. "Go get Crimmins. Now!"

He turned to the second man. "David, find Albert Mitchell. Bring him here. We need us a lawyer." David moved toward the door.

Morgan was pounding on the inside of the storeroom door. "Open the door, dammit, Lyle. That bastard's got my son."

"I'll open it, but you got to promise to listen to me if I do."

"Open it, Lyle!"

"You gonna listen to me?"

Henessey cringed when he heard glass breaking. "Lyle, less you want every damn jar and bottle in the place broken, you open the goddamned door."

Henessey shook his head. "Alright, alright, I'm coming." Another crash echoed through the store as Henessey moved behind the counter and reached under for his gun. He unloaded it, dumped the shells in his pocket, and closed the cylinder.

Stepping back to the door, he reached for the bar just as Morgan began another assault. "Come on, Lyle, dammit!" Something else made of glass crashed against the door. The shards of the wreckage cascaded down the other side of the door as Henessey pulled the bar free.

The door flew open and Morgan charged straight into the barrel of Henessey's Colt. He stopped, a stunned look on his face, but he didn't back up.

"You gonna use that, Lyle?"

"If I have to, yes. You ready to listen to me?"

"If I have to, yes."

"Alright, simmer down, then. I got people after Tate Crimmins and Albert Mitchell. We got to wait until they get here."

"What for? Crimmins won't do anything. You told me that yourself."

"He will if I push him hard enough. We've had enough, Morgan. This ain't going to go no further. You have my word on that."

"Unh hunh. And who's Mitchell?"

"He's a lawyer."

"Tom doesn't need a lawyer. I don't need a lawyer, either. I need my gun."

"I'm trying to tell you we can handle things without that, Morgan. Don't be so damned pig-headed."

"No you can't. Kinkaid wants me, and he's about to get what he wants."

"And then what?"

"I'll worry later."

"You listen to me now, you don't have to worry later."

Morgan was about to argue when Crimmins appeared in the store's front door. "Lyle, what the hell's going on?"

"Tate, your man Kinkaid's finally gone and done it."

"Done what?"

"He's beat up Tommy Atwater and thrown him in jail."

"Tommy? What for?"

"Because he's trying to get to me," Morgan said.

"But he can't do that. He . . ."

"You ain't listening to me. He's done it, Tate. What we got to do is undo it. And I'm telling you right now, we *are* going to undo it. First we are going to get Tommy out of jail. Then you are going to tell Kinkaid his services are no longer required in Cross Creek. We can't wait for the federal marshal. I want you there because you're the father of this mess. You can help clean it up."

Crimmins seemed reluctant. Morgan and Hennessey realized at the same moment that Crimmins was afraid of Kinkaid. "No excuses, Tate. He's gone, as of now, and that's that."

"What about the contract?"

"You do what you want. As far as I'm concerned, he broke it a long time ago. I should have done something sooner. But I won't wait no more,

I'll tell you that. He about killed Morgan's boy, and I think it's our fault. I *know* it is. I got David Ray running down Albert Mitchell. We are going to do this according to the book. Albert will see to that."

Crimmins lapsed into silence. Henessey was right and everyone in the store knew it. Morgan reached into his pocket and fished out a key. He flipped it to Ben.

"Go over to the hotel," he said. "Room five. Get my gunbelt."

"Morgan, I told you, you don't need your gun. We've had enough gun play as it is."

"Lyle, I appreciate your concern. I really do. But I've been dealing with this all my life. I know what it's like, and you don't have a clue. I want my gun." He turned to Ben. "Go get it, Ben, please."

Ben stood there, the key in his outstretched hand. He looked at Henessey, then at Morgan, then back at Henessey. "Go ahead, Ben," Lyle said. "And be quick about it."

Crimmins cleared his throat. "You think you can take Kinkaid, Atwater?"

Henessey exploded. "Damn it, Tate! Didn't you hear what I just said?"

"I heard you, Lyle. But I'm asking him, not you. Can you, Atwater? Can you take him?"

"I don't know."

"He's plenty fast, I seen that often enough," Crimmins said.

"Tate, what's your point?"

"My point is, what if Kinkaid don't want to be fired. We stir him up, we got a hornet's nest on our hands. I don't think that's such a good idea. I was wondering could Atwater handle the situation. If it comes to that, I mean."

"No you weren't, Tate. I know you. You don't think like that. Now, what were you getting at?"

Crimmins cleared his throat and was about to explain when David Ray and Albert Mitchell arrived. He waited impatiently for the situation to be explained to Mitchell, then he turned to Henessey again.

"Go on, Tate," Henessey said.

"Well, it's like this." Crimmins was stalling for time. "Kinkaid's a gunfighter. And we're all pretty much agreed that he's out of control. But Atwater, here, he's a gunfighter, too. I was just thinking . . . we owe Kinkaid the rest of his pay. By contract, I mean. Albert, you done the papers, ain't that the way it is?"

Mitchell nodded. "That's true," he said.

"So, I was thinking, if Atwater takes care of Kinkaid, we can just pay him the money. He can be the new marshal or he can not. Whatever he wants. It won't cost the town anything extra, either way."

"Is that it, Tate?"

"That's it."

Atwater took two quick steps and planted himself squarely in front of Crimmins. He grabbed the front of the mayor's vest and tugged it up under his chin. "You big tub of guts. I never took money in my life to shoot a man. You understand me? Never. And I ain't about to start now. You make me sick. It's men like you make men like Brett Kinkaid possible. You plant them and you tend them, you water and feed them, just like they was some kind of precious flower. But it isn't like that. Not at all." He shoved Crimmins and the banker stumbled back until he slammed into the counter. The impact rattled the change in the cash drawer. It was the only sound in the store, except for Morgan's raspy breathing.

He started toward the door as Ben stepped up onto the boardwalk. He snatched at the gunbelt and buckled it on. He checked the cylinder, and put a shell in the empty chamber. The gun slid in and out of the holster once, then again. The shallow thud of steel on leather punctuated a whispered conversation between Henessey and Mitchell.

Morgan rapped on the door frame. "I'm going to get my son," he said. "You can come along or you can wait here. I don't give a damn."

He started out the door, and Henessey called after him, "Hold on, Morgan. We're coming."

Atwater was already moving up the block by the time the rest of them made it through the door. Henessey started to run, and he caught Morgan three quarters of the way to the marshal's office. Brett Kinkaid lounged in the doorway. His jacket was already pulled back behind his right hip.

"Morgan, try it my way first, please? It's the best way. You know it is."

"I want my boy, Lyle. I don't care how I get him, but I want my boy. And if he's as busted up as you say, you better get a doctor over here. One way or another, we're gonna need one."

Kinkaid hadn't moved. Henessey watched him with one eye while he despatched David Ray to find the doctor.

Morgan stepped to the front of the marshal's office. Henessey bulled in front of him, pinning Morgan behind him with outstretched arms.

"Gentlemen," Kinkaid said. "Nice day for a walk. A little hot, though, ain't it."

Henessey looked back for Crimmins. The mayor was shuffling along behind the rest of the men, and Henessey shouted, "Tate Crimmins, you get your ass over here. Now."

"That's the mayor you're talkin' to, Lyle," Kinkaid said.

"I know damn good and well who it is. You shut the hell up, you understand me?"

"Lyle, I am not in a particularly good mood. I had a troublesome morning, and when I get like that, I get impatient."

Kinkaid moved away from the door frame and watched as Crimmins reluctantly came forward to stand beside Henessey.

"Marshal," Crimmins said.

"Mr. Mayor. You got something to say to me?"

"You tell him, Tate. Damn you. Tell him."

"You have Tommy Atwater in jail, do you?"

"Yes, sir, I do."

"Let him out, dammit."

"Can't do that. It wouldn't be right."

"I've had enough," Morgan said, twisting away from Henessey's grip.

CHAPTER 20

Albert Mitchell joined the small knot collecting in front of the office. "Mr. Kinkaid," he said. "What are you charging the Atwater boy with?"

"Hell, I don't know. Public nuisance, obstructing justice, whatever."

"What's his bail?"

"Bail? He ain't got no bail. It ain't been set. Need a judge for that. No judge in town, you know that."

"That's right, there isn't. But as mayor, Mr. Crimmins is authorized to function in such matters. He is a magistrate, and he can handle it."

"I don't know anything about that."

Crimmins looked at Mitchell. "I didn't know that," he said.

"Just do it, Crimmins," Morgan snapped.

Crimmins cleared his throat, once, then a second time. His voice sounded strangely thin, as if his collar were too tight. "Ten dollars. That about right, Albert?"

Mitchell nodded.

"I got the money," Henessey said. He reached into his pocket and pulled out a wallet. "Ten dollars?" He counted out the bills and handed them to Crimmins. Then he turned to Kinkaid. "There, now let him go."

Mitchell stepped up onto the boardwalk. Henessey followed him. Kinkaid squared up, blocking the door. "Where the hell you think you're going?" he asked.

"We're going to get Tommy Atwater," Henessey said. "You got no reason to hold him, now. Get out of the way."

"Don't you think his father ought to be the first one to see him? Seems like if he can't afford to pay to get him out, the least he could do is be the one to pick him up."

Morgan stepped onto the boardwalk. "I'll get him," he said.

"Through me, though. Ain't that the way it's supposed to be, Morgan? Ain't you supposed to go through me?"

"No. That's not the way it's supposed to be. I'm through with that."

"You disappoint me, Morgan. It's plain to see you're nothing anymore."

Morgan swung and caught Kinkaid by surprise. The punch landed in Kinkaid's mid-section, and he doubled over, falling backward into the office. Morgan was on him in a flash. He jerked Kinkaid's gun free and threw it out into the street, then he propelled him on through the door. Kinkaid landed in the dirt. He lay there stunned as Morgan turned to move back into the cell block.

Henessey rushed in after him, snatching the keys from a wooden peg over the door. He unlocked the cell and yanked the door open, then stepped back to let Morgan inside.

Tom still lay unconscious. His left arm was draped, palm down, over his face. The back of the wrist was covered with dried blood. His neck and the front of his shirt were bloody, the dark stains already beginning to flake on the skin and peel away. Morgan knelt beside the cot, reached up for Tom's hand, and pulled it away gently.

When he saw Tom's face, the nose flattened where he had been kicked, the ugly gash under one eye, and all the blood, he cursed. Tom's eyes had been blackened, and both cheeks were swollen. He groaned as Morgan moved the limp arm to one side. "Tommy? Can you hear me? Tom? It's me, Mor... it's Dad. Are you alright?"

Tom groaned again, and his head flopped to one side, but his eyes didn't open.

Morgan got to his feet. "That sonofabitch," he shouted. "Where is he?"

He started back through the cell block as the doctor stepped in. He knocked the doctor to one side as Henessey clawed at his back. "Wait, Morgan, hold on, now. Just wait, dammit."

But Morgan was in no mood to wait. He barreled through the front door and out onto the walk,

Henessey right behind him. A crowd had begun to gather, and they buzzed excitedly as Morgan stepped into the street.

He walked up to Crimmins and shook him by the shoulders. "Where is he?"

Crimmins shook his head. "Don't know. He just left. He ..."

Morgan shoved him aside. Someone pointed toward Largo's, and Morgan started to run.

"He took his gun," Crimmins shouted.

Morgan ignored him. He stood in front of Largo's and shouted, "Come on out, Kinkaid."

There was no answer. Morgan bent to pick up a rock and threw it under the swinging doors. "Kinkaid! Kinkaid, come on out."

He stepped toward the walkway, feeling that awful tension between his shoulders. It came down to this. The thing he wanted to avoid, the thing he had tried to hide from, and to outrun, and to pretend had never been. But he couldn't avoid it. There was no place to hide, and it was too fast for him. It was his life, and he would have to live it this way, whether he wanted to or not.

Morgan picked up another rock and tossed it into the bar. He saw a shadow just inside the doors and a second later one boot. But it wasn't Kinkaid. The boot was plain, and dusty, not the fancy Mexican leather Kinkaid wore. A second later the doors started to move and a burly man wearing an apron burst outside.

"He's in there," he said. "Kinkaid's in there."

"Tell him to come out."

"He won't do it. Says you should come after him."

Morgan knew better. He wasn't going inside. If Kinkaid wanted him, he would have to come out. In a loud voice, he said, "I don't have time for this bullshit. If he doesn't have the guts to come out, that's fine with me."

He started back, never taking his eyes off the door. Kinkaid would not be able to resist. He knew that. Too much was riding on this. If Kinkaid quit now, he would be unable to face himself. He'd rather die than cut and run. And Morgan realized that he didn't care which choice Kinkaid made. For the first time in his life, it wasn't important. There were things that mattered, that meant something. But this wasn't one of them. Brett Kinkaid wasn't worth it. He could crawl back under whatever slimy rock he called home, and that would be just fine.

But he knew it wasn't going to be that easy. He knew it had gone too far for that. He was nearly thirty yards from the walk in front of Largo's when he heard a voice calling from inside the bar.

"Come back here, you yellow bastard. Don't you walk away from me. Atwater? You hear me? Don't you walk away from me."

Morgan saw the doors swing open partway, then swing shut again. He stopped. And waited.

In the gap under the door, he could see the fancy boots. If he wanted to, he could drill Kinkaid through the door. But he wouldn't and somehow Kinkaid knew it. The prisoner of some warped code that both men understood and only one followed any longer, he knew Morgan wouldn't shoot him. Not that way.

The doors swung open again, and Morgan heard the hush fall over the buzzing crowd up the street. Kinkaid, his jacket still smeared with dust from where he had fallen in the street, brushed the doors aside with his elbows. He stepped onto the walkway, and the doors clacked twice as they swung shut behind him.

"You were going to walk away from me, weren't you, Morgan?"

"Yes, I was."

"Afraid to die?"

Morgan shook his head. "No, Kinkaid, I'm not afraid to die. But I'm not afraid to live anymore, either. But you are. That's why you won't let this go."

"Ain't you the poet, though. You getting religion, Morgan? Seems like this town's already got enough ministers."

Morgan shrugged. "It doesn't have to be this way, Kinkaid."

"Oh, Morgan, but it does. It *does* have to be this way. You know that. Deep down inside of you, deep in that yellow gut of yours, you know it's got to be this way. I knew it as soon as I laid eyes on you. And then, when I got that newspaper and the picture, I knew it wouldn't be long."

"You shouldn't have taken it out on my boy."

"Hey, I had to do something, Morgan. You weren't cooperating."

"Maybe you read too many dime novels, Kinkaid."

"Hell, I'm gonna be in one, soon as we're through here."

"You think so?"

"Got to be." He walked down into the street. His jacket still covered his gun butt, and he brushed it back with a practiced maneuver. Morgan tensed for just an instant, but he knew Kinkaid wasn't ready. He had to talk himself into it awhile yet.

"Remember that feeling at the back of your neck you were talking about, Kinkaid? You got it yet?"

"Yeah, I got it."

"Because I can see your cheek twitching. You're not ready for this, Kinkaid. This time you're on the other end."

"Nice try, Morgan. But you can't fool me. I'm not afraid of you."

"You should be."

Kinkaid snorted. Then, like a father sadly disappointed in a favorite son, he shook his head slowly from side to side. "I'm not, Morgan. I'm really not."

And he made his move. He was fast. Morgan saw the blur of Kinkaid's hand. But this was not something he had any control over. He had been through this so many times, he couldn't have stopped if he wanted to. He felt the weight of his Colt as it cleared the holster. He felt the texture of the trigger under his finger. He felt the kick back against his thumb as the gun went off.

Kinkaid's gun barked once, then again. Something slammed into Morgan's shoulder, spinning him to the left. He went down on one knee as

Kinkaid fell. The marshal lay on his back and Morgan struggled toward him, his gun ready, but unwilling to shoot again if he didn't have to.

But Kinkaid wasn't going to let him off that easily. He sat up, braced on one elbow. "Told you it was going to happen, Morgan," he said. His hand tensed around his pistol. Morgan saw it, and fired. The bullet slammed Kinkaid back onto the ground. One leg twitched spasmodically, shaking his whole body.

For some reason, Morgan saw only the fine mist of beige dust slide off Kinkaid's jacket, shaken loose by the spasm. He glanced at his arm, and saw where the sleeve had been sliced by one of Kinkaid's bullets, felt the sting of the plowed flesh. There was a lot of blood, but the bullet hadn't struck any bone.

He holstered his gun and turned to look up the block. Henessey was racing toward him. "You alright, Morgan?"

Morgan nodded. Crimmins waddled toward him, a hand outstretched. "Thanks, Atwater," he said. He had a wad of bills in his other hand, and he thrust them toward Morgan.

When he saw the money, Morgan reached out, took the bills, and balled them in his fist. Then he stuffed them down inside Crimmins's vest. "No thanks," he said.

He turned to Henessey, "How's Tom?"

"He's got to mend some, but he'll be alright."

"I guess you'll be leaving my employ," Henessey said.

"Like hell I will, Lyle. You don't get rid of me that easy. I got a life to lead, and I might as well do it here. If my family won't mind."

"Somehow, I don't think they will."

Bill Dugan is the pseudonym of a full-time writer who lives in upstate New York with his wife and daughter. This is his third western for Harper Paperbacks.

HarperPaperbacks *By Mail*

ZANE GREY CLASSICS

THE DUDE RANGER
0-06-100055-8 $3.50

THE LOST WAGON TRAIN
0-06-100064-7 $3.99

WILDFIRE
0-06-100081-7 $3.50

THE MAN OF THE FOREST
0-06-100082-5 $3.95

THE BORDER LEGION
0-06-100083-3 $3.95

SUNSET PASS
0-06-100084-1 $3.50

30,000 ON HOOF
0-06-100085-X $3.50

THE WANDERER OF THE WASTELAND
0-06-100092-2 $3.50

TWIN SOMBREROS
0-06-100101-5 $3.50

BOULDER DAM
0-06-100111-2 $3.50

THE TRAIL DRIVER
0-06-100154-6 $3.50

TO THE LAST MAN
0-06-100218-6 $3.50

THUNDER MOUNTAIN
0-06-100216-X $3.50

THE CODE OF THE WEST
0-06-100173-2 $3.50

ARIZONA AMES
0-06-100171-6 $3.50

ROGUE RIVER FEUD
0-06-100214-3 $3.95

THE THUNDERING HERD
0-06-100217-8 $3.95

HORSE HEAVEN HILL
0-06-100210-0 $3.95

VALLEY OF WILD HORSES
0-06-100221-6 $3.95

WILDERNESS TREK
0-06-100260-7 $3.99

THE VANISHING AMERICAN
0-06-100295-X $3.99

CAPTIVES OF THE DESERT
0-06-100292-5 $3.99

THE SPIRIT OF THE BORDER
0-06-100293-3 $3.99

BLACK MESA
0-06-100291-7 $3.99

ROBBERS' ROOST
0-06-100280-1 $3.99

UNDER THE TONTO RIM
0-06-100294-1 $3.99

MAIL TO: **Harper Collins Publishers**
P. O. Box 588 Dunmore, PA 18512-0588
OR CALL: **(800) 331-3761 (Visa/MasterCard)**

Yes, please send me the books I have checked:

❏ THE DUDE RANGER (0-06-100055-8)	$3.50	❏ THE CODE OF THE WEST (0-06-100173-2) $3.50
❏ THE LOST WAGON TRAIN (0-06-100064-7)	$3.99	❏ ARIZONA AMES (0-06-100171-6) $3.50
❏ WILDFIRE (0-06-100081-7)	$3.50	❏ ROGUE RIVER FEUD (0-06-100214-3) $3.95
❏ THE MAN OF THE FOREST (0-06-100082-5)	$3.95	❏ THE THUNDERING HERD (0-06-100217-8) $3.95
❏ THE BORDER LEGION (0-06-100083-3)	$3.95	❏ HORSE HEAVEN HILL (0-06-100210-0) $3.95
❏ SUNSET PASS (0-06-100084-1)	$3.50	❏ VALLEY OF WILD HORSES (0-06-100221-6) $3.95
❏ 30,000 ON HOOF (0-06-100085-X)	$3.50	❏ WILDERNESS TREK (0-06-100260-7) $3.99
❏ THE WANDERER OF THE WASTELAND		❏ THE VANISHING AMERICAN (0-06-100295-X) $3.99
(0-06-100092-2)	$3.50	❏ CAPTIVES OF THE DESERT (0-06-100292-5) $3.99
❏ TWIN SOMBREROS (0-06-100101-5)	$3.50	❏ THE SPIRIT OF THE BORDER (0-06-100293-3) $3.99
❏ BOULDER DAM (0-06-100111-2)	$3.50	❏ BLACK MESA (0-06-100291-7) $3.99
❏ THE TRAIL DRIVER (0-06-100154-6)	$3.50	❏ ROBBERS' ROOST (0-06-100280-1) $3.99
❏ TO THE LAST MAN (0-06-100218-6)	$3.50	❏ UNDER THE TONTO RIM (0-06-100294-1) $3.99
❏ THUNDER MOUNTAIN (0-06-100216-X)	$3.50	

SUBTOTAL .... $_____

POSTAGE AND HANDLING .... $ ___2.00*___

SALES TAX (Add applicable sales tax) .... $_____

TOTAL: $_____

*ORDER 4 OR MORE TITLES AND POSTAGE & HANDLING IS FREE!
Orders of less than 4 books, please include $2.00 p/h. Remit in US funds, do not send cash.

Name _____

Address _____

City _____ State _____ Zip _____

(Valid only in US & Canada) Allow up to 6 weeks delivery. Prices subject to change.   HO301